TIDELAND

TIDELAND

A Novel by
Mitch Cullin

Dufour Editions

First published in the United States of America, 2000
by Dufour Editions Inc., Chester Springs, Pennsylvania 19425
This paperback edition published 2006
Reprinted 2007, 2013

© Mitch Cullin, 2000

Cover Design by Andrew Kelly

ISBN 978-0-8023-1340-9

The Library of Congress catalogued
the hardback edition of this title as:

Cullin, Mitch, 1968-
    Tideland : a novel / by Mitch Cullin.
        p. cm.
    ISBN 0-8023-1335-3
        1. Poor girls--Fiction. 2 Fathers and daughters--Fiction. 3.
    Texas--Fiction. I. Title.

PS3553.U319 T53 2000
813'.54--dc21   00-027918

Printed and bound in the United States of America

For Mary and Barbara

AUTHOR BIOGRAPHY

Mitch Cullin is the author of the acclaimed novels Whompyjawed and Branches. Besides being a featured author at the Texas Book Festival, he has been the recipient of many awards and honors, including a Dodge Jones Foundation grant; writing sponsorship from Recursos De Santa Fe; the Stony Brook Short Fiction Prize; and a nomination for inclusion in the American Library Association s "Notable Book List, 1999." His fiction has appeared in The Santa Fe Literary Review, Christopher Street, The Bayou Review, Austin Flux, Harrington s Gay Men s Fiction Quarterly, and other publications. His story "Sifting Through" appeared in Little, Brown's Best American Gay Fiction 2, and an excerpt from his forthcoming novel–Cosmology of Bing–is featured in Alyson's Gay Fiction at the Millennium anthology. He currently resides in Tucson, Arizona.

Thanks to the following for support and inspiration:

Amon H., Bill H., Bill O., Brian B., Burt K., Chad P., sisters
Charise and Chay and the girls, Charlotte R., Cole T., F & Z
& Y, Horton, Jemma, godson Jesiah, John N., Martin and
Judith and Renee, Max E., Mr. Mifune, Mom, Moon &
Brown Star, Nez, Peter C., Pete T., Richard B., Robert P.,
brother Steve, Strummerville, Thomas L.–and, of course, Lai
Lai Dumpling House, Betos, and Velvet Elvis Pizza. Lastly
and most importantly, much love and mega-nods to Brad
Thompson and my father Charles Cullin.

The dead and the sleeping,

how they resemble one another.

–Gilgamesh Epic

One

1

On my first evening in the back country, I skipped down the porch steps of the farmhouse–leaving my father inside and the radio playing and my small suitcase decorated with neon flower stickers unpacked–and wandered toward the upside-down school bus I'd spied from an upstairs window. Flanked on either side by Johnsongrass taller than my head, I followed a narrow and crooked cattle trail, extending my arms straight out for a while so my palms could reach into the grass and brush against the sorghum.

"You bend so you don't break," I whispered as the Johnsongrass slapped across my hands, half-singing the song my father had written about me: "You bend so you don't break, you give and you give, but you can't take, Jeliza-Rose, so I don't know what to do for you."

And I continued along the trail for some time–winding left, then right, then left again–until it ended at a grazing pasture sprinkled with foxtails and the last bluebonnets of late spring. A breeze shuffled through the humidity, and the sky was already dimming. But the low-growing bluebonnets were still radiant, so I carefully stepped over them while moving further into the pasture.

Behind me swayed the Johnsongrass.

Before me rested the upside-down bus in a heap–the hull a mess of flaking paint and seared metal–with most of the windows busted out, except a few which remained black and sooty. It seemed bluebonnets had sprouted everywhere, even from under the squashed bus roof, where they drooped like bullied children. And the air was so rich with the scent of lupine that I sniffed my fingertips as I came to stand beside the bus, inhaling instead an earthy odor which belonged to my filthy dress.

The bus door was ajar, an inauspicious entryway. Peering within, I spotted the melted steering wheel, the upholstery on the driver's seat bursting fuzz and springs. A smoky scent filled my nostrils, bubbled plastic and corrosion. And even though I was eleven, I had never been in a school bus. I had never been to school. So I squeezed past the inverted door, glancing at the stairwell overhead, and delighted in the glass chunks crunching beneath my sneakers.

Looking through the topsy-turvy windows, I shook a hand at the Johnsongrass outside, pretending they were my parents waving from a sidewalk somewhere. Then I put myself below a seat in the rear, imagining a busload of fresh-faced kids filling the other charred seats, all smiles and chatter, smacking gum, spinning paper airplanes down the aisle, and I was leaving with them.

From where I sat, the second floor of the farmhouse was visible, jutting behind the high Johnsongrass. The upstairs lamp was on, glowing in the third gable's window. At dusk, the old place no longer appeared weathered and gray, but brownish and almost golden–the eaves of the corrugated steel lean-to reflected sunlight, the thumbnail moon hung alongside the chimney.

And soon the grazing pasture erupted in places with bright soft intermittent flashes, a lemon phosphorescence. The fireflies had arrived, just as my father said they would, and I watched them with my dry lips parted in wonder, my palms sliding expectantly on the lap of my dress. I felt like running from the bus and greeting them, but they joined me instead. Dozens of tiny blinks materialized, floating through the smashed windows, illuminating the grim bus.

"I'm Jeliza-Rose," I said, bouncing on my crossed legs. "Hello."

Their flickers indicated understanding: The more I spoke, the more they blinked—or so I believed.

"You're going to school. I'm going to school today too."

In vain I reached out, attempting to snatch the nearest one, but when I unclenched my fist there was nothing to be seen. After several failed captures, I made myself content by simply naming the fireflies as they flashed.

"You're Michael. You're Ann. Are you Michael again? No, wait, you're Barbie. And that's Chris. There's Michael."

The bus was suddenly populated by children of my own creation.

"We're going on a great trip today," I told them. "I'm as excited as you are."

The sun had almost disappeared. And if the train hadn't startled me so, I might have stayed in the bus all night, lost in conversation with the fireflies. But the train flew by without warning, rattling the ground, and making me scream. I had no idea that tracks were concealed in thick weeds beyond the pasture, perhaps fifty feet away, or that each evening at 7:05 a passenger train tore past the property.

For a moment it seemed as if the world had started spinning faster. A vagrant wind pushed into the bus, mussing my oily hair. Squinting my eyes, I noticed blurs of silver and fluorescence outside, glimpses of people riding in the coaches and dining car, followed by freight cars—and then the caboose, where a lone figure seemed to be waving from the cupola.

Then the train was gone—so were the fireflies, having been whisked afield by the wind. I was alone again, still screaming, terrified. I bit my bottom lip without thinking, felt the skin crack, and tasted the blood as it swam onto my tongue. And everything became quiet, just the faint breeze whooshing the tall reeds, three or four solitary crickets tuning up for the night.

I glanced in the direction of the old house, knowing my father was in the living room, quiet and awaiting my return. Then I studied the rows of Johnsongrass, which had grown darker during dusk. That's where the Bog Man is, I thought, wiping blood from my lip. And I knew I'd better leave the bus before it got too late. I had to be with my father before the Bog Man stirred.

I needed to unpack.

2

When I entered the living room, my father was exactly how I'd left him earlier–consumed in an opiate trance, shoulders straight, hands gripping both knees, boot heels flat and even on the floorboards. In a high-backed leather chair, he sat facing a wall, wearing his big sunglasses, which always reminded me of the Lone Ranger's mask.

"That'd make you Tonto," he often told me at home in L.A. "My little girl's a Hollywood Injun."

"I'm not Tonto," I'd say.

"So who are you then?"

"Don't know, but not Tonto."

And that would make him laugh. He'd grin, maybe pat his fingertips back and forth over his mouth, going, "Woo woo woo," like a TV Indian.

Sometimes I joined him, dancing around the apartment and hooting until the cranky woman downstairs banged a broomstick on her ceiling.

But that night at the farmhouse, my father's jaw was set, his face firm with two wizened lines incapable of producing a smile. So I didn't bother mentioning the Lone Ranger, or the school bus, or how the train had frightened me. I didn't say anything, preferring instead to stand quietly beside the chair and scrape my front teeth across my cracked lip, a pleasing discomfort.

Nighttime had shaped the living room, making it shadowy and strange. Without sunlight coming from the windows, fixing bright angles along the floor, climbing up nooks, the place no longer felt welcoming. Even after flicking the overhead light switch—bringing on a hazy bulb that hummed with electricity—I'd sensed some change in the surroundings when tiptoeing toward the chair, like moving through a gauze-like mesh but not quite seeing or feeling it.

And the sight of my father gazing at the wall, where his tattered map of Denmark was tacked, brought to mind the Bog Man photograph he once showed me at the apartment. It was past midnight, and he shook me in my bed, saying, "Listen, you should know this before I forget. Bog water has weird powers. These bodies get lain in bogs for thousands of years and don't decay. I mean, they get a little brown and shrunk and stuff, but not much else."

Then he held open a library book and pointed at a black-and-white photo: an Iron Age man in the course of excavation, my father explained, removed from nine feet of peat, his head covered by a pointed skin cap, around his waist a hide belt.

"The book says he got murdered two thousand years ago," he said, exhaling bourbon-breath.

So I propped on an elbow, blinking tiredly, and studied the well-preserved remains of the boney Bog Man, who was stretched on damp soil as though sleeping, the arms and legs curved, his chin inclined. His face displayed a benign expression—the eyes gently shut, the mouth puckered.

"They killed him?" I said.

"Hanged him and stuck him in some bog in Denmark. You're looking at someone deader than dirt."

"Who killed him?"

"Who knows," he said, slapping the book shut. "But let's

hope we're in that kind of shape in two thousand years. That's what I wanted to tell you."

Then he gave me a sloppy kiss on the forehead, saying I'd better go back to sleep, otherwise my mother and all the bog men in the world might get upset. And as he reeled from the room, I asked for the light to stay on.

"Sure, baby," he said, "you got it."

But the light didn't help much. The picture had spooked me, and I couldn't rest for hours.

Several nights later, I dreamt the Bog Man materialized in my bedroom and tried suffocating me with a pillow. A noose encircled his neck, drawn at the windpipe, coiling like a snake on his chest. And as he bent forward with the pillow, his wrinkled brow and pursed mouth carried a look of affliction. I suppose the nightmare made me shout out, because when I stirred, my father was stooping over me, brushing hair off my face, a length of which I'd somehow sucked back into my throat.

"What's all this?" he said, half-whispering. "Got the creepers?"

Then he lifted me from the sheets.

I wrapped my arms about his collar line, buried my head against his T-shirt, and he carried me to where my mother slept. And I remember thinking there wasn't a bog man alive who could mess with my father.

But at the farmhouse, the map wasn't the only thing that recalled the Bog Man—it was my father's stoic face, all creased and furrowed, unflinching, as if preserved from antiquity in a jar. His long black ponytail, fastened by a rubber band, draped across his right shoulder and hung down the front of his tank top. At sixty-seven, almost forty years older than my mother, his body was lean, his arms brawny and taut. In the stillness of the living room, it was easy to conjure an Iron Age man in his image: frozen in a leather chair, excavated intact, the pupils behind those big sunglasses locked forever on a map of Denmark s geognostic conditions.

"Let me tell you two something," he said one morning during breakfast, speaking in his slow Southern drawl.

My mother and I were sitting with him at the dining table, a rare occasion when the three of us were awake at the same hour.

"A secluded and private life in Denmark is where we're headed. I've got it into my head."

After performing all night, playing two different clubs in West Hollywood with his band The Black Coats, he had arrived at the apartment holding a bag of bacon, egg, and cheese biscuits from McDonald's.

With a grimace, my mother lowered her biscuit, saying, "What's in Denmark? When you ever been there anyway?" She glanced at me and said grumpily, "Where does he get these crappy ideas?"

It was a question not meant to be answered, so I kept eating in silence.

Half-frowning, he said, "I'm just thinking we could move and get a place without a phone. Nobody would know we was there, so if somebody wants to hound me, they won't find me or you or Jeliza-Rose."

"I won't go," she said, swallowing her last bite, "so don't bother trying. It's stupid."

"Hey, whatever you want," he replied. He didn't look at her, or at the uneaten biscuit on his plate, but stared straight at me and winked. "Guess me and Jeliza-Rose will make the trip. How's that, huh?"

I shrugged and smiled with my mouth full.

She pushed her chair back.

"Noah, you and the shit-critter can go whenever you like. I don't care."

Her robe fell open as she stood, so she shrugged it off, letting it drop to her feet. And the chunky whiteness of her naked body quivered when she left the table.

My father leaned forward and whispered, "Your mother is the Norse Queen Gunhild, King Eric Bloodaxe's widow. And King Harald promised to marry her, enticing her to Denmark, and so she went—but on her arrival she got drowned in a bog instead. Not very nice."

"No," I said, "not very nice."

"Think she deserved it?"

"No."

"No," he said, considering his biscuit, "I suppose she didn't."

His shoulders went slack and his stubbled chin wavered above his plate.

The day my father and I finally escaped the city, he said we were headed for Jutland soil. In his backpack was the map, which he'd torn from a library book. And as we began traveling east on a Greyhound bus, watching palm trees and apartment complexes skim by our tinted window, my father produced the map and flattened it on his legs. With a shaky finger, he pointed out our aim—the western Jutland, where bog men slept under great, unbroken plains.

Then he carefully folded the map, returning it to his backpack, and said in an abstracted murmur, "I see before me these dark banks, decorated with the creator's most beautiful flowers, Danish men and women, greeting the May sun as it rises to the east. I hear them greet it with songs, with freedom's folksongs. The Danish beech, the Danish waves echo the jubilant tones."

And I knew he was about to fade out, as he usually did after taking his Fortral tablets, a painkiller that kept him walking—or so he liked to say. But I didn't care. I was glad to be going somewhere else. I was happy Queen Gunhild couldn't make the journey, even if Texas, not Denmark, was our final destination.

On the first evening at the farmhouse, I put myself between my father and the map on the wall, asking, "Daddy, is Jutland like Texas?"

But he was gone, so talking became pointless. His breathing had grown shallow. And I was sleepy.

Going from the living room, I pictured myself as Alice, growing tired as she dropped down, down, down the rabbit-hole. It was my favorite part of Alice s Adventures in Wonderland:

After such a fall as this, I shall think nothing of tumbling down-stairs! How brave they ll all think me at home!

I often asked my father to read that section again and again, and he'd make his voice higher, sounding somewhat like a girl, saying, "Dinah'll miss me very much to-night, I should think!"

"Dinah was her cat," I told him.

"I hope they'll remember her saucer of milk at tea-time. Dinah, my dear! I wish you were down here with me! There are no mice in the air, I'm afraid, but you might catch a bat, and that's very much like a mouse, you know. But do cats eat bats, I wonder?"

"And here Alice began to get rather sleepy, and went on saying to herself, in a dreamy sort of way–"

"Do cats eat bats? Do cats eat bats?"

"And sometimes–"

"Do bats eat cats?"

"For, you see, as she couldn't answer either question," I said, having memorized every word, "it didn't matter which way she put it. She felt that she was dozing off, and had just begun to dream that she was walking hand in hand with Dinah, and was saying to her, very earnestly–"

"Now, Dinah, tell me the truth: did you ever eat a bat?"

And that night in the farmhouse, I headed upstairs with Alice on my mind.

She wondered if she'd fall right through the earth, imagining how funny it'd be to come out among the people with their heads downwards. She'd have to ask them the name of their country–New Zealand? Or Australia? Of course, it wouldn't be Denmark, because that wasn't on the other side of the rabbit-hole.

3

My single mattress lacked sheets. So did the double-bed where my father had tossed his backpack. Our upstairs rooms were separated by the only bathroom in the house, though there was no running water. And the empty toilet bowl released an acrid stench when the lid was lifted, as if rotten eggs festered somewhere deep within the plumbing.

My father said the place needed a new well. He said there was plenty of work to be done.

"The yard wants some tending," he mentioned during our second afternoon of Greyhound travel. "Mother had this boy mow and weed when she was living, but I suppose that fellow is all grown by now. And there's nails coming up on the porch, so I guess we can hammer them. Squirrels lived in the attic, but I got rid of them because they kept chewing the wiring and everything. They made a real racket in the morning, and I hated knowing they were there. But Mother liked them. She said the place didn't feel so lonesome that way."

It's true, the farmhouse seemed imbued with a lonely quality—no doubt due to its isolated location. And I often wondered why my father let his mother live on the property by herself. He had purchased the land for her in 1958, right after his third guitar-instrumental single "Jungle Runner" reached the Top Ten. The house was built several years later, and Grandmother remained there until 1967, when she tripped down the porch steps, breaking her hip, and died in a nursing home soon afterwards.

"Thought about putting the place on the market then," my father told me on the bus, "but my second wife talked me out of it. And now I'm glad she did."

For him, the farmhouse became a retreat, somewhere to hide and make music. He had the phone disconnected, got rid of Grandmother's television. By the time I turned eleven, it was common for my father to leave the city for a few months, taking his Rickenbacker guitar and driving east in his Buick Riviera. Only once did he invite my mother and me, but my mother said, "Fuck that, Noah. Texas is the armpit of the universe. We'll be here when you decide What Rocks can exist without you."

It was Grandmother who named the farmhouse What Rocks, but I'm not sure why. She was dead before I was born, so I never had a chance to ask her. Perhaps it was a joke of some sort, considering the nearby quarry existed as a constant nuisance; every other day or so there was dynamite blasting, which disrupted the sense of isolation, booming like thunder and rattling the windows.

"When I bought it for her," my father explained, "I told her she could sell it off someday to that quarry if she wanted. I'm thinking she could've made a little dough, you know, selling the limestone under that property. But I don't think she ever considered doing that. I mean, the house and land were a gift, so that'd have been rude in her mind. She was a pretty proper old woman sometimes, wouldn't even drive this baby-blue Cadillac I got her because she thought it looked too showy. I tell you what, we could sure use that car today."

Riding in the Greyhound made my father restless. The seat aggravated his spine, which was damaged when he slipped headlong from a stage in Chicago, landing squarely on his back. But being on the run, he couldn't afford any other mode of transportation. His prized Buick Riviera with white sidewalls was traded for a sandwich bag of mixed pills—Pamergan, Dextromoramide, Diconal, DF-118, Fortral, and Methadone, my mother's favorite. And when we finally arrived in the small town of Florence, some ten miles from the farmhouse, he uttered a low groan while putting on his backpack.

Then he handed me my neon suitcase, saying, "Suppose you're ready for a picnic."

"Pizza," I said, earnestly.

"Can't eat pizza on a picnic," he said. "You should know that."

"We don't have to have a picnic," I said, following behind him as we moved along the passageway.

"Got to eat sandwiches. That's what you eat. That's what it's going to be."

At the Main Street grocery store, whatever cash remained went toward saltines, Wonder Bread, peanut butter, and two gallon jugs of water. And even though some minor celebrity status was attached to his name, my father's face was far from well-known. It was like a black-and-white Western where the gunslinger saunters into the saloon; soon as we stepped through the doors—a grubby little girl and a pale, long-haired man wearing huge sunglasses—all heads turned toward us, all mouths stopped talking.

It wasn't as if the store was crowded. In fact, I recall just a chubby bagger boy with a crew cut and two high school-looking checkout girls, one Hispanic, the other white, both sporting hair-sprayed bangs that curled upward like a wave.

"What time is it?" my father asked.

"S-s-sorry, not wearing a w-w-watch," the boy replied, stuttering painfully, his lips and jaw twisting spasmodically as he spoke. "Around four, I-I-I think."

"It's about four-thirty," the Hispanic girl said.

"Then you're still open."

"Until five. Six on Saturday."

"That's good," my father said, taking my hand. "Where's the peanut butter?"

"Center aisle, near the marshmallows, to the left."

And when we returned to the front with our groceries, my father asked the bagger boy if he knew someone who might give us a lift.

The checkout girls glanced at each other, their grins verging on laughter.

"Where you-you-you g-going?"

"East of town, out toward the microwave tower on Saturn Road."

"Guess I-I-I could t-t-t-ake you," the boy said, unfolding a paper sack. "It's on my w-w-ay home, if you don't mind waiting till I-I-I'm off."

"Not at all," my father said. "I appreciate it, friend."

The afternoon sun had colored the asphalt golden, and as the bagger boy drove us from Florence in his Nissan pickup, he put on a pair of dark convex glasses–less against the bright rays spilling across the county road, I suspected, than against my father's menacing eyewear. His name was Patrick.

"I live with my g-g-g-grandfa-fa-father," he explained, accelerating the vehicle. "We're going fishing to-to-to-tonight, so I-I-I'm in a bit of a h-h-h-urry."

Then he asked if we were visiting family, wondered where we were traveling from.

"Going to see my parents," my father lied. "My girl and I live in Austin."

I was sandwiched between them in the cab, my knees on either side of the gear shift.

"Th-th-that right," Patrick said. "Austin's gr-gr-great! Haven't had much of a ch-ch-chance to know people a-around here. Just moved from D-D-Dallas. Not from Florence. My grandfather's b-b-b-been here for-e-e-ever."

"Forever's a pretty long time," my father said.

"You bet-bet-bet-cha," Patrick sputtered. "I-I-I think I-I-I-I'd go nuts if I-I-I stayed here as long as he-he-he has."

And while Patrick struggled in conversation with my

father, I tucked my shins underneath my butt, pushing myself up, and gazed over the dashboard at the hilly landscape ahead. Cedar and mesquite trees grew along the road, in pastures lush from spring thunderstorms. This was farming country. In the distance, the microwave tower my father had mentioned loomed like a futuristic obelisk, reddish girders crisscrossing, an infrequent strobe flaring at its top.

My father told Patrick to turn on Saturn Road, and soon the pickup was bouncing across a winding dirt road. "How f-f-far?"

"A mile or so, maybe two. First gate you come to is good enough. That's pretty much it."

The microwave tower was now in the rearview.

To the left, dense groupings of cedar.

To the right, a clear meadow under a canopy of low-lying clouds.

Then we passed empty sidelots parceled by barbwire fences, each with a real estate marker advertising new concepts in family living, reasonable financing available. The wild grass had been grazed or chopped down, but was still thick enough for snakes and armadillos to hide in.

"Tons of d-d-deer out here," Patrick mentioned. "Rain has g-g-g-given them e-e-e-nough to eat."

The pickup flew past longhorns sunning themselves beneath a windmill.

"An hour or two before the sun's gone," my father uttered, turning to stare as we zoomed by.

When Patrick pulled off at a long frame gate, he asked, "This it?"

"Yep," my father replied. "Awfully kind of you."

"No p-p-problem."

We climbed from the truck and began organizing ourselves. With his backpack hanging off a shoulder, my father clutched the grocery sack against his chest. I was slightly lopsided, gripping a gallon jug in one hand, my suitcase in the other. Chalky road dust, stirred up behind Patrick's Nissan, caught us and then billowed on.

Patrick mentioned that once a week he did a delivery run near What Rocks–to let him know if we needed anything–and, leaning across the cab to close the passenger door, he said, "H-h-have a nice one."

My father gave him a nod, and I smiled but he didn't seem to notice. He was already shutting the door. Then he had the pickup bumping around in the opposite direction, sending more sandy dust to the air, and sped away.

The purr of cicadas rattled among the mesquite and cedar trees. From the road, What Rocks wasn't visible, only the thick Johnsongrass which grew wild on the property. "Go on," my father said, planting a boot against the bottom cord of barbwire alongside the frame gate. He pressed the cord to the ground, creating a wide gap.

So I crossed under the range fence, and he followed, grunting with exasperation as he bent. Then the two of us walked to the washed-out driveway, each occupying a gravelly rut.

"Weeds get the better of everything," he said, mumbling to himself.

He glanced at me, elaborating, "When there's no cattle on the land, the weeds grow greedy."

About a half-mile in, where the driveway forked between two cedars, the farmhouse came into view.

"Wow," I said, trudging toward my father, who had stopped near one of the trees, "is that What Rocks?"

"That's her," he said, wiping his brow with the heel of his palm. His backpack was at his feet, the grocery sack crumpled and torn beside it.

I set my suitcase and the jug on the ground, keeping my eyes on the old place.

A flagless flagpole stood in close proximity to the wrap-around porch. There was a copper-colored weather vain on the lean-to, but shaped as a grasshopper instead of a rooster. And while it appeared no different than most two-story farmhouses in Texas–pitched roof and an open plan–its weathered planks, gray and stark and splintering, gave it a decidedly forlorn facade. Even before stepping through the doorway, I sensed the layers of grime, frayed spiderwebs, crumbs, and mice droppings that were eventually found within.

"Home at last," my father said, sounding somewhat relieved. He hoisted his pack, unzipped the top, and rifled inside, producing a shoelace with a key tied at the end.

And in less than three minutes, I was already upstairs in What Rocks, staring from my bedroom window at the upturned school bus, while my father was downstairs tacking up the map of Denmark.

Night arrived.

I had been to the bus and returned. Now I was upstairs again, having left my father in the living room. On the edge of the single mattress, where a faded brown stain filled the middle, my suitcase sat open. Carefully, I removed what few items I'd managed to pack—my mother's satin nightgown, and an armful of Barbie doll parts (four heads, two arms, one torso, six legs, each dismembered piece unearthed in a thrift shop bin). Aside from the contents of the suitcase, another thrift shop purchase, my dress, panties, socks, and sneakers were all I had.

Biting my sore bottom lip, I took a moment ordering my possessions. The nightgown, which had been folded haphazardly, was given rest on the mattress pillow, a regal flourish in my imagination. The doll parts were then arranged in a line beside the pillow: heads first, then arms, then legs, then torso.

Finally, I zipped the suitcase, noticing with some sadness that its neon-colored flower stickers were coming unstuck, and shoved it underneath the bed anyway. And while crouching, a tiny drop of blood spattered on the floorboard. So I drooled into a palm, watching as a red string of saliva formed in my cupped hand.

"I'm dying," I said in mock-horror, affecting the voice of a soap opera actress. "I can't go on, I must go on."

I went to look in the bathroom mirror. Puffing my bottom lip, I spotted the sliver of split flesh oozing blood, but was disappointed it wasn't any worse. So I spat at the sink, hoping my spit would suddenly turn crimson and profuse. It didn't. In fact, it seemed mostly clear.

"You will survive," my reflection told me, aping a TV doctor. "A complete recovery is expected."

"Thank you, thank you," I replied. "Now there's hope."

Then I twisted the sink knobs, praying a little water might spurt out so I could brush my teeth. But nothing happened. It didn't matter anyway, I reasoned, because I'd forgotten a toothbrush and toothpaste. And when I brought a finger to my clenched teeth, sliding it back and forth like I was brushing, more blood bubbled from my lip.

My reflection grinned, showing me how the blood had discolored the crowns.

"You're red all over," I said, noting my orangish hair and freckles, the hyacinths on my dress.

"Simply ghastly," my reflection exclaimed in an English accent, just then catching music playing faintly in my father's bedroom. "A ghastly noise, Jeliza-Rose."

"Yes, we must put an end to it," I replied, turning from the mirror.

Then I crossed to the other bathroom door, which opened into the adjoining sleeping quarters.

When I entered, the hinges creaked like in some monster film, so I stood near the doorway for a bit, sucking my bottom lip and taking everything in—the backpack on the bed, the lamp glowing on the night table, the ratty throw rug on the floor. My father's room was almost identical to mine, except he had a double mattress with a larger stain. On the windowsill above the headboard, a hand-held radio transmitted music girl, you really got me going, you got me so I don t know what I m doing—and I remembered how my father kept the radio pressed against an ear as the Greyhound journeyed through the desert, listening with his eyes shut, sometimes sleeping for hours while music or news or static droned.

"You really got me, you really got me," I sang, going to the mattress.

The contents of his backpack were in a small pile on the

bed, unwashed clothes topped by a depleted Peach Schnapps bottle. The sandwich bag once containing the mixed pills had been emptied, and was now stuck over the bottle neck like a makeshift prophylactic. And I pictured my father swallowing and swallowing and swallowing, then exhaling relief as he waited for the hallucinations and thought disturbances to begin. "Thought disturbances–" that was what he called them, "sweeping clean the little messes in my brain."

I climbed across the mattress toward the windowsill. Parting the curtains, I saw the strobe flutter from the distant microwave tower.

Then I saw nothing.

The world outside was darker than I ever knew it could be. And aside from the strobe and several moths trying to thump past the pane, it seemed as if all else had fallen into a vast hole. There was just me and my father and What Rocks and the radio. The Johnsongrass had disappeared. So had the horizon.

Imitating Patrick the Bagger Boy, I stammered, "I-I-I think I-I-I'd go nuts if I-I-I stayed here as long as he-he-he has."

Then I took the radio from the windowsill and carried it from my father's room.

4

I was naked with my arms stretched over my head. My dress was on the floor, covering my sneakers and socks, and the hand-held radio sang the blues on my night table. My mother's nightgown, all shimmery pink and smooth, sank around me. And I could smell her, the persistent body odor she often had. The gown was so massive over me that for a moment I was lost underneath it—my hands searched for the sleeve openings, my head rummaged against the silk in an effort to reach the neckline.

The headless housewife, I imagined, flapping her arms like a chicken.

When I finally poked through the collar, my hair stood on end with electrostatic. Then I scrunched the sleeves past my wrists, and tried twirling in a circle like a dervish. But the gown was too long, so I had to stop.

"You're crazy," I told myself, grabbing the radio. "You're insane."

"That's right, looks like any chance we had for rain has all but disappeared," a throaty-sounding DJ said, speaking over the fade-out of a song. "Well now, instead of thunderclaps here's Mr. John Lee Hooker—as requested by Jimmy in Salado—going boom boom boom for everyone on the Stillhouse Hollow Lake marina."

Ah-boom boom boom, I wanna shoot ya right down!

With John Lee Hooker vibrating in my hand, I headed downstairs. The gown dragged at my feet, and it was a precarious trip from one squeaky step to the next. Still, I managed without trouble, envisioning myself as a graceful ghost while descending into the murky dining room. At the bottom of the stairs, the gown hem swept across the floorboards, stirring dust in my wake. But it didn't matter much. Everything was dusty anyway—the long dining room table, the oak sideboard, the air I inhaled.

"Aaaa-choo!" I faked a sneeze, hoping to summon my father's attention.

To the right of the stairs was the kitchen, and to the left was the dining room and then the living room, separated by only a wood-burning stove. Because the entire downstairs lacked interior walls, it was fairly easy to gaze from room-to-room—especially when standing at the foot of the stairs.

"Aaaa-choo!" I went again, but my father remained as before in the living room, so I about-faced and glided into the kitchen.

Leaving the radio near the stove, I dug in the grocery sack and placed the goods on the counter. Then I turned ravenous.

A saltine dabbed into the peanut butter jar, breaking the glossy surface.

More saltines followed.

John Lee Hooker had long since finished, and now bluegrass music entertained the kitchen. Wild fiddles and stomping feet kept time with my smacking.

I drank from a gallon jug, spilling water on the gown.

Then my index finger became a knife, squishing peanut butter across a slice of Wonder Bread. And I continued eating and drinking, waiting for my stomach to feel satisfied.

By the time I was full, my eyes had grown tired. There was peanut butter on the roof of my mouth, along the ridges of my gums, and I was content, half-awake and nourished, listening to "K-V-R-P, eclectic music for eclectic minds—"

Fatigue pushed me downward.

With the gown bunched over me like a blanket, I was aware for the first time how very warm What Rocks was—as if the entire place was holding a stifled breath. But the floor seemed cooler than anywhere else in the house. And the radio was now playing Tumbleweed, one of my father's slower songs, so it was okay to rest for a little while.

In the ethereal moments before sleep, I imagined my father on a stage in some L.A. dive, where a beam of indigo light shone on him, glistening in the creases of his black leather pants and jacket. With his legs apart, his guitar held in front of him like a weapon, he curled his top lip, saying, "This is for the loves of my life, my baby girl and my beautiful wife."

An Elvis moment, he called it. Every performance needs one.

Tumbleweed, tumbleweed blowin cross the yard
Wonder where you re goin , wonder how far
Tumbleweed, tumbleweed rollin in my mind
Wonder what she s doin , wonder who she ll find

My mother bragged that the lyrics were written about her, and I never heard my father say otherwise. He wrote them while touring England during the early '70s. That's where they met. My mother, a runaway from Brooklyn, was a wafer-thin eighteen-year-old, who had an Asian guru named Sanjuro. She also had The Who, or, to be exact, the drummer, Keith Moon. By then, my father was a guitar-twang icon, known for his string of instrumental hits in the 50's, and an emotive, ferocious style of playing that had influenced a young Pete Townshend. Evidently though, when Pete saw my father perform in London, he was quite disappointed. It was an acoustic performance of country standards, mostly Hank Williams and Johnny Cash covers. Following the show, Pete went backstage long enough to shake my father's hand, then he sulked away by himself.

"I'm sure he made a song about that night," my father once remarked, digressing from how my mother was introduced to him. "'The Punk Meets The Godfather'—I'm positive that one's about me. Not a nice tribute."

But Moon the Loon was delighted.

"I won't say I don't like country," he exclaimed, "because I do!"

He had arrived in my father's dressing room disguised as an orthodox Jew, reeking of brandy and hyperbole.

"Musical innovation, a step forward backwards," he cheered maniacally. "Just like Mozart, except different! A Gordian Knot in a shoelace!"

And as a gift, he ushered forth my mother—"an insane bint for your pleasure and gratuity"—who waltzed into the dressing room costumed as Pippi Longstocking. She looked tomboyish, tall and slender, with the cheeks of her face freckled and her blue eyes shining.

"Don't know if it was love at first sight," my father had said on the Greyhound, "but pretty darn close, I think. And it was good to begin with, and it stayed good for a long time because she made me feel like a kid—and I still had some money then. And she knew where to get diamorphine cheap, so I saved some dough because by the time we met I'd been buying expensive Chinese heroin. But she could get me brown and medical heroin for much less than what I'd been paying for the Number 4 type. Your mother was connected, Jeliza-Rose. Even when we moved to LA, she knew who to call and where to go. And before she got lazy and fat she could cook us up a storm. She made burritos and pizza and all kinds of greasy nice stuff. I miss that about her. I wish you'd known her then. She really was a treat."

But he might as well have been talking about someone else. My mother slept all day and ate Crunch bars for dinner and talked to herself until dawn. And she wasn't a treat.

I can't say when it was exactly that I began to hate her, but I suppose it started after I turned nine. By that point, my parents were full-time junkies. My father was incapable of touring, and he had grown emaciated and weak. My mother, on the other hand, had ballooned in weight–so much so that on the rare occasions when she managed to climb from bed, the springs creaked as if groaning relief, and the mattress continued to sag with the impression of her body.

At nine, I was given two chores–massaging my mother's legs, sanitizing and preparing the syringe. And while I became conscientious at both, there was only enjoyment to be had in making sure the needle was ready. Because my father believed public education bred dumb children, I was schooled at home, which amounted to little more than stolen library books (literary classics picked by my father, way beyond my reading ability), and afternoons of PBS.

Soon as I awoke in the mornings, my first class began in the kitchen–where concentrated bleach was drawn into the syringe from a coffee cup, then squirted away in the sink. After the process was repeated, I flushed the syringe and needle through with cold water. Next, I scooped some junk from its hiding place in a sugar tin, dissolving the brown dust in a teaspoon with hot water and vitamin C powder. Then using a dining table chair for a perch, I stood at the gas stove, holding the spoon over a burner, feeling the stainless steel warm as the flame helped bubble clean the remaining particles.

Once the solution was safely sucked up into the syringe, I carried my homework to the living room. My father would either be sitting on the floor with his guitar or stretched across the couch gazing blankly at the television.

Sometimes he'd say, "Good morning," while taking the syringe from my hand. But usually he said nothing.

He just targeted the large vein running the length of his inner arm, injecting himself, then–in the brief moments before the rush seized him–brought the remaining amount to my mother in their bedroom.

After the morning ritual, I was pretty much done until evening. My recess lasted hours. I was free to watch TV, and–by organizing the dining table chairs, collecting the dirty clothes and sheets strewn around the apartment–I erected an elaborate tent home in the living room. There I ate quiet meals in the company of my Barbie heads.

For breakfast it was two Eskimo Pies from the freezer. For lunch I alternated between Pop Tarts and Nutter Butters. Dinner consisted of Dr. Pepper, a Milky Way, cinnamon toast.

But, if all the Milky Ways were gone, I'd substitute one of my mother's Crunch bars, which were supposed to be off limits. And even though she spent weeks in the bedroom, somehow she sensed when I'd been at her candy; while rubbing her feet at night, I always paid for the transgression by receiving an abrupt kick on the chin.

"What have I told you before?" she'd say again and again. "You miserable creep, you never learn! I can't teach you anything about what's mine!"

But I had learned something: heroin gave my father neutrality, serving as an antidote for a mind too difficult to manage. For my mother, having lived a short life lacking much meaning at all, heroin offered nothing. The drug had run away with her as a teenager, and the experience was ultimately a mediocre one. Her warm, dreamy, carefree bubble had become a void. So, when going to her bedside, I knew who the real miserable creep was. And I knew she would eventually kick out, or throw the wet rag she used to wipe the sweat from her puffy face. Still, she never struck hard enough to make me cry. Mostly, she just ranted. Sometimes making sense, often not.

While massaging the fatness of her pale legs, pushing my fingertips along the lumpy skin, my mother's mouth seemed to function independently of her brain. "Lip-smacking junkie baby," she called me, and I understood a verbal barrage was about to follow. It seemed scripted, differing slightly with each performance: "Withdrawal is what I went through–that way you wouldn't get born hooked. Irritable and hyperactive baby too, nothing but a high-pitched cry and twitching and spasms and convulsions. Your daddy blew smoke in your mouth to keep you quiet, you know that? Think you got damaged by that, but don't blame me. Because I breast-fed you forever—and they're all wrong, dear, because drugs don't mess with breast milk in a major way. It's your daddy's fault you're like you are. Not mine. I loved you."

Taking a labored breath, she dabbed the rag to her forehead and then propped up on her elbows, the bedsprings squeaking as she did. Her voice suddenly changed, becoming softer.

"Jeliza-Rose, do you know I love you? Honey, I'm sorry. If you'd just fix me a hit and something to eat, I'll do something nice for you soon. I promise, baby."

I always played my part too, nodding, fully aware of the lie—she would never do anything nice for me soon. But leaving her bedside, I'd manage a smile anyway, tormented by the thought of ever entering that bedroom again, or of touching her swollen calves.

So on the afternoon she turned blue and died of respiratory failure, I skipped around the living room whistling the theme from Sesame Street, the happiest song in the world.

"The methadone killed her," my father said, looking haggard and confused on the couch. "I should've kept her on junk—just cut her daily dose and kept her on it."

Junky logic: with the hope of finally getting clean, he had traded the Buick for pills—though he understood that methadone was more addictive, more dangerous, and more deadly than heroin.

Bringing his hands to his face, he said, "Now she's dead, and I don't have a car."

A week earlier, he and my mother had decided to quit mainlining. The tough decision came after our apartment was robbed late one night. I remember waking to the sounds of the front door splintering and breaking open, my father shouting, "Get the fuck out of here! I said I'd get the dough Thursday! Talk to Leo, that's what I told him!" There were other voices, men with calm and threatening tones, saying, "Listen, Noah, we've been through this," and, "No more screwing around, all right?"

But in my bed, I pretended it was all a spooky dream.

When I stirred the next morning, I found my father in the kitchen. He was pouring the contents of the sugar tin into the sink. His hands were shaking, and his teeth chattered, even as he said, "Howdy, sweetheart."

The microwave was missing. So was the toaster.

In the living room, the TV and VCR and stereo were gone.

"Bog men paid us visit," he told me. "But now we're okay. I've talked with your mother. It's all good. You'll see."

And I started crying–not because I was glad or relieved, but because the very idea of bog men dragging themselves into the apartment filled me with horror.

My father set the tin aside. "Oh, no," he said, "everything's fine." Then he tried lifting me, but couldn't gather the strength. So he hugged me instead, patting my neck, saying, "See, when was the last time Daddy did this? It's getting better already." I felt his fingers trembling, the sweat on his palms. "Not a thing to worry about, my little girl." And I almost believed him.

But on the day my mother's corpse rested in their bedroom, it was my turn to be the comforter. Her overdose had taken about twelve hours to run its course. What began as irregular breathing, concluded with blue skin and pupils reduced to a pinpoint, but all the while my father expected her to pull through. In a last effort to revive her, he poured cold water on her face, but it didn't help.

"Please don't be sad," I told him in the living room, putting my head against his shoulder. "We can go to Jutland if you want."

For a moment he grinned. "Wouldn't that be wonderful."

"Yes," I said, "and we can eat her Crunch bars too."

Then he held me close, saying, "No one's taking you from me. That's not happening here. We're leaving, okay?"

"Okay."

While I quickly packed, my father swaddled my mother from head to toe in the bedding. Then he called me to join him in their bedroom.

"If she was a Viking ship," he announced, "we'd have to

bury her with horses and food and gold plates."

He wore his backpack and seemed anxious to get going. I stood beside him with my suitcase, staring at the shrouded corpse. Even in death, her body odor was potent. "Anything you want to say?"

I shrugged. "I don't know. She's like a mummy."

He sighed.

"Well, I've pretty much said what I wanted when she was alive, so no point wasting time."

He dug his Bic lighter from a pocket, clicked on the flame, and attempted to ignite the mattress. But it wouldn't catch, so eventually he gave up, saying, "Bad idea anyways. It might burn the whole building and everyone else."

And as we hurried from the bedroom, I paused to take a final glance at my mother, imagining her congested breathing while dying. Her pulmonary arteries had become clogged with blood, forcing the fluid through the capillaries and into the lungs. In the violent throes near the end, she kicked her chubby legs wildly, shaking the bedsprings to the limit.

"Come on," my father said. He was waiting at the end of the hallway. "Don't stare, it's bad luck."

"Mom's dead all right," I said, turning to face him.

Gripping my suitcase, I thought, Poor Queen Gunhild– drowning in a bog like that.

5

It was still night when the mystery train appeared. The whistle entered my dreams, manifesting itself as a doorbell buzzing.

Waking on the kitchen floor, I listened while the freight cars flurried alongside Grandmother's property, picturing the school bus shaking in the pasture. Soon the whistle grew fainter until the only sound came from the portable radio, a female DJ reading the news: "A mixed message from the White House, conflicting with earlier statements—"

I rubbed my eyes and yawned. Then I sat up, squinting around the kitchen.

The jug was on the counter without its cap. Cracker crumbs dotted the floor. The gown remained damp in spots from my reckless guzzling. But my throat was dry, and while licking at the sore lip, I tasted peanut butter instead of blood.

"A miracle," I whispered, sensing the creamy substance coursing in my veins. And if I hadn't felt so suddenly alone, I would've laughed at the thought of being a Peanut Butter Girl, just flesh and bone and crushed edible seeds.

Climbing from the floor, I called out, "Daddy—? I'm in the kitchen!"

The gown hem lagged under my feet, so I pretended it was the soles of satin slippers and shuffled to the stove. Then taking the radio in hand, I shuffled out of the kitchen, through the dining room, and into the living room.

"Daddy–? I was in the kitchen. Daddy–?"

As if roused by a rooster's crow, I was hoping my father would be awakened by my voice. The vacuousness of his face, head, and posture would vanish. He would quickly rise from the chair. But standing before him with the radio, I noticed only a small difference in his appearance. In the dreary light of the living room, his lips had grown purple, his breathing had ceased. Lifting the big sunglasses, I was met with an icy stare– two pupils reduced to almost nothing–so I lowered the sunglasses back over his eyes.

"I brought you this," I told him, putting the radio in his lap. Then I crouched before his boots, bending my legs inside the gown, and gazed up the expanse of his stiff body.

"Three are dead in a college motor coach crash," the DJ reported. "The motor coach, packed with college cheerleaders from the University of Texas in Austin, flipped over near Georgetown yesterday, killing the coach and two cheerleaders. Seven others were injured, four critically. The accident is under investigation."

Just then I recalled my father on the Greyhound, holding the radio against an ear, listening to similar news broadcasts. "They'll be searching for me," he told me. "I need to monitor the information as it develops." But during our trip, there was no mention made of him or my mother's corpse, a fact which somehow disappointed him. "Seems I don't matter much anymore, Jeliza-Rose," he later said. "Not worth a lousy headline."

And squatting there by his boots, I wanted to tell him how much he mattered to me–how it was good being at What Rocks with just him, even if it wasn't really Denmark. Then tears welled uncontrollably under my tired, heavy eyelids.

"It's not your fault she's dead," I said. "She wasn't very nice anyways."

"Now don't get all weepy," I pictured him saying. "Everything's fine."

But it wasn't fine, and I told him that.

"It's awful!"

I crumpled across his boots, my chest heaving.

"It's all right," he'd tell me. "You're safe as houses."

I imagined his hands stroking my neckline, soothing.

Exhausted again, I began to drift off. And before sleep overtook me, I conjured the Bog Man in his bed of peat. His bones gnashing as he dug himself from the earth. But on my first night in the back country, the idea of him was no longer so frightening.

"He survived thousands of years," my father once said. "He just lay there waiting to come back to life."

"Please, come back to life," I pled, dimly aware of the radio wavering on my father's lap, the batteries loosing power as my eyes closed. "Please—"

The wind was now blowing around What Rocks, sweeping along the porch, clanking the hoist rope against the metal flagpole. The old place shuddered. In the pasture, the school bus rocked gently, the high Johnsongrass wavered. Thunder rumbled in the distance. But inside I slept once more, the wind droning in my dream like a horn—and somewhere the mystery train whistled for no one as it chugged through barren and forbidding terrain, weaving further and further away from us.

6

I yawned with the feeling that dawn was just beginning, but the sunbeams descending through the windows, slanting crosswise on the floorboards, told me otherwise. The living room was warm, full of radiance and shadow. Rays had already fallen across the lower half of my gown, where my toes fidgeted in the dusty light. "Morning, morning," I muttered to myself, lifting my head from the boot tips, an uncomfortable pillow.

Then I stood quickly, pivoting on bare heels to my father. "Good–morning."

Skin that had grown pale was now completely pallid. But his earlobes, chin, forearms, and fingertips were discolored with a reddish-purple stain. It seemed that overnight the stiffness had left his body. The rigor around his lips and nose had vanished, giving him a sagging, almost benign expression. In the daylight, he was limp, his muscles no longer controlled anything. For a moment I held his hand, cautiously peering at his sunglasses. He wasn't cold. In fact, his temperature was equal to the warmth of the room. And a stubble had begun growing on his cheeks.

But I wasn't too worried. He'd done this before: back at the apartment, he'd sometimes sit in front of the TV for days, statuelike, or he'd curl up on the couch and sleep and sleep and sleep. Then he'd suddenly stir. He'd climb from the couch, make himself coffee and something to eat, and be all smiles again. So once I asked, "Were you dead?"

And he replied, "Sugar, nothing can kill me. Daddy was only on vacation. That's what I do, your momma too. We're playin' possum, you know?"

Playing possum for days, while I waited with my toys and watched TV and wondered when they'd return. And they always did. Except now Mom was really dead; I knew that for certain. But not my father—he was playing possum again, vacationing in Denmark or somewhere else. Anyway, people didn't just sit down and die. They rolled around sweating and screaming and dying. Like on TV, they gasped a lot while bleeding, or they fell to the ground in pain. They held their sides and kept their eyes open until, at last, they were gone. On TV, I'd seen people die a million times, and they never just sat down and stopped. They didn't play possum or go on vacation. They died—like Mom.

"Are you on vacation?"

Instead of waiting for an answer, I grabbed the silent radio from his lap, bringing it to my ear. I turned the volume dial back and forth, moved the station meter from one end to the other and back. Nothing worked. So I returned it to him with a sigh.

"Because if you're not," I said, "then it's not funny then."

I wanted to rage around the living room, pounding the floorboards in frustration. But the urge to pee was so bad that my insides hurt.

"Won't talk to you too," I told him. "It's not nice, you know. You won't like it too."

Then I left indignantly, pausing only to struggle from the gown, and hurried naked out the front door.

Beyond the porch, a clear sky stretched above the Johnsongrass. And while maneuvering past corroded nail caps that jutted from the planks, I squinted in the sunlight, which landed hot on my legs and stomach. Going down into the yard, I squatted beside the bottom porch step, and began urinating in the weeds. The piss came in a gush, spattering my ankles. Eventually, a small puddle formed underneath me, and I had to move my feet further out so they wouldn't get wet.

When the pee dwindled, I glanced up with intense relief—and to my astonishment, a doe stood no more than twenty feet from where I hunched. She had wandered from the Johnsongrass with her long neck crooked, grazing at the nettles on the ground. At first I was so startled by the sight of her that I couldn't think what to do. But finally I took a deep breath, pushed upright, and said, "Hi, are you hungry?"

Her head shot up, ears twitching, and her big eyes fixed on me. Keeping my gaze locked on her, I stooped and yanked at the stems of several weeds, all having been wetted by my urine. Then I went forward, carefully putting one foot in front of the other, offering the uprooted weeds in an open palm. But as I approached, she bolted. That's when I spotted her left hind leg dangling at the joint, as if the bone had somehow been snapped at the femur.

"Don't go!" I yelled, watching as she sprang into the Johnsongrass, the bad leg straggling, and disappeared on the cattle trail. "Come back!" I shut my palm, crushing the weeds, then threw them at the ground. "Stupid, I got you food!"

I considered bounding after her. If she knew how fast I can run, I thought, she'd be my friend. Then I could feed her and pet her and bring her into the farmhouse so she could sleep. I imagined hugging her in the kitchen, where she'd heal with the gown tied on her leg like a silky bandage. But when I heard the scampering, jabbering racket coming from behind, the idea of pursuit faded.

As I spun around, the noise stopped abruptly. Putting my hands above my brow, I scanned the porch. But nothing unusual presented itself. So I tilted my chin back, looked at the awning of roof that hung over the porch, and found myself eye-to-eye with a gray squirrel; he was frozen in place with a bushy tail curling near his head, studying this naked child in the yard below: "I see you," I said, grinning. "I know you're there. You can't hide."

With his tail darting, the squirrel chattered at me briefly, an incomprehensible and irritated sound. On the edge of the awning, he made skirting movements left and right, freezing each time to give me an askance stare, then ran nimbly across the roof, scurrying to the east end of What Rocks. I followed in the yard, scratching my thighs on the overgrown buckthorn that had sprouted from under the porch.

"What were you saying?" I asked.

Reminding me of Spiderman, the squirrel sprinted along the exterior wall, traversing the wooden siding with tentative stops and starts. He halted beside the upstairs window of my father's room, where a wide knothole existed. And even though the hole appeared too narrow, the squirrel squeezed halfway in, chattered some more with his rear section and tail sticking out, then slipped through with no effort.

"You better wait," I said, hoping he might hear me and return. "I didn't understand you."

Because the knothole was by the window, I pictured the squirrel exploring my father's room, rummaging in the backpack on the mattress, sniffing at the empty Schnapps bottle. And I recalled a documentary my father and I once saw on PBS, which showed how clever squirrels could be–hanging upside down from branches and stealing bird-feeder seeds, sailing between trees in order to avoid elaborate lawn traps set by angry homeowners.

"Pigeons without wings," was what my father called them.

Sometimes the two of us took long walks alongside the L.A. River. When we reached Webster Park, he delighted in chasing pigeons from our path, kicking at them with his boots. But if my father hated pigeons, he hated squirrels even more.

"They're like rats," he explained. "They'll chew on anything, practically eat metal. Not worth shit. At least you know where you stand with a rat."

"I don't think I like rats," I told him.

"Well, I don't like squirrels," he said.

As a boy, a squirrel he'd captured in a milk crate bit him. "Broke the skin on my thumb so bad I could've bled to death. Me and my cousin beat it dead with a bat, but not before it tried climbing my pants leg, all crazy and mad. I swear that sucker meant to do me harm. Then for months afterwards I kept getting these really horrible dreams–squirrels all over my bedroom, in my bed, gone totally nuts, tangling themselves in my hair, sinking those big yellow teeth deep in my scalp, tearing at everything. It was awful."

And on those afternoon walks, my father often picked a nice-sized rock from the ground. Then we'd leave the path and go behind a bush, huddling in anticipation. Soon as a squirrel wandered into view, he'd leap forward, pitching the rock like a baseball player. Usually he missed, but on at least three occasions a squirrel was struck, sending it rolling over in the grass.

"Gotcha," he said, almost laughing as the stunned rodent struggled to its feet. "Look at the poor dumb thing!"

Standing directly beneath the upstairs window, I knew my father would hate the idea of a squirrel lurking somewhere in the farmhouse.

"You'll get in trouble," I shouted at the knothole, "so you shouldn't be in there!" It became apparent that the squirrel wasn't listening, so I rushed onto the porch, once again minding the nail caps, and went inside.

While passing the living room, I said to my father, "I'm not telling you a secret because you won't like it."

Then I skipped to the stairs, thinking that if the squirrel was hiding in What Rocks, I'd need some serious help. In my bedroom, I wondered which Barbie head would join me. Contemplating each piece on the mattress, the decision was easy. Magic Curl Barbie head, with her thick blond hair, lacked guts. Both Fashion Jeans Barbie head and Cut 'N Style Barbie head were damaged–someone had stabbed a hole in Fashion Jeans' right eye, Cut 'N Style's forehead and eyes had been colored black with a pen. My choice was Classique Benefit Ball Barbie head, my favorite, and the only one to have real rooted eyelashes.

Planting Classique's head on my index finger, I said, "Are you ready?"

"Of course," she replied, "I was born ready."

"Good, because this could get pretty dangerous."

"How wonderful."

Creeping into the bathroom, we hesitated by the door to my father's room. "I'm scared," I whispered. "What if he tries to bite me?"

"Nonsense. You're a big girl. A squirrel is only a squirrel."

"I know," I said, turning the knob. "But you go first."

The hinges squealed as I pushed the door open. And before going in, I made certain the squirrel wasn't hanging above the doorway, ready to drop on my head. Then I extended my arm, entering with Classique leading the way.

"See there," she said. "Safe as houses."

Everything was as before–the dirty clothes and Schnapps bottle, the backpack, the lamp on the night table, the throw rug on the floor.

"But I'm sure he's here," I said, walking forward.

I had expected to find the squirrel waiting on the mattress, upright on his hind legs, teeth flared, paws punching in my direction.

"Don't be so sure, dear."

We leaned, peeking under the box spring, spotting dust balls, a folded section of newspaper, the exoskeletons of several June bugs. Then we crawled across the mattress, where I examined the windowsill, searching for the other side of the knothole.

"Where does it come out?"

"Beats me," Classique said. "Maybe he's magic. Maybe he isn't really a squirrel at all but a fairy."

I pressed my nose against the wood paneling, sniffing like a bloodhound for any sign of the squirrel. A strong butternut smell filled my nostrils, almost producing a sneeze. So I turned my head, easing an ear against the paneling, and listened.

"Not even as good as a pigeon," I said.

"Unless he's magical. That's what he was telling you, I think."

"Maybe," I said, catching a bustling patter within the inner wall. "Do you hear that?"

"I think so."

"He's in the wall," I said, tapping an area left of the windowsill. "Classique, he's right in here." And as I tapped harder, the stirring quit.

Then I heard chattering.

Then silence.

"What do we do now?"

"If you want my opinion," Classique said, "I think you should get dressed. If you put clothes on, you won't frighten the animals away."

"You're right," I said, suddenly self-conscious.

"I know," she replied.

Returning to my bedroom, I put Classique with the other Barbie heads, then scooped my dress from the floor, saying, "I don't believe in fairies. Only lightning bugs are like fairies anyway, not squirrels. Squirrel butts don't glow, just lightning bug and fairy butts."

Once the dress was on, I sat at the edge of the mattress, cradling the socks and sneakers in my lap. The socks stank, so did my feet.

"Frito feet," I called them, inspecting the brown undersurface of my right foot. Then, before pulling on the sneakers, I whiffed the frayed insoles, recoiling from the sharp aroma.

"Gross," I said, snorting a laugh. "Spaghetti cheese."

And suddenly my stomach rumbled. The Peanut Butter Girl needs breakfast, I thought. Then I remembered my lip. I searched for the slit with my tongue, but couldn't locate it. So dragging my shoelaces across the floor, I headed into the bathroom for a better look.

In the mirror above the sink, I turned my lip down.

"Stop pouting," I told myself, trying to sound like my mother.

The cut had all but healed, so I crossed my eyes for a second, growling at my reflection: "You're hopeless, Jeliza-Rose. What are you good for? You can't even keep bleeding?"

Then I knelt to tie my sneakers. And while knotting the laces, I noticed a small hatch below the sink, fashioned from the same wood as the wall panels. It was kept shut by a night latch which had become speckled with rust.

In my imagination, the hatch was the door Alice unlocked in the rabbit-hole, opening to reveal a corridor that ended at a garden, where beds of bright flowers and cool fountains existed. And because the entry was bigger than what Alice had discovered, a DRINK ME potion wasn't needed for shrinking.

"Classique," I shouted, using both hands to pivot the bolt from its notch, "there's a way in!" The other end of the knothole, I thought. Squirrel, you can't hide from me.

As the hatch swung ajar, a humid draft rushed out, bringing the scent of sawdust into the bathroom. From where I crouched, it was impossible to tell what lay beyond the hatch, except a murky space illuminated by an insubstantial amount of natural light. There was no passageway to be seen, no garden, no squirrels drinking from fountains.

So I went and got Classique, who said, "Bring Magic Curl with us. She can help."

"Are we going in?" I asked, sticking Magic Curl on my pinky.

"I think so, dear. I don't see why not."

"I don't want to go," Magic Curl said. "This isn't a good idea."

"Shut up, you baby," Classique snapped at her. "You're not going in with us, you're just keeping guard."

"Why can't Fashion Jeans or Cut 'N Style do it?"

"Believe me, I wish they could," Classique said. "But both your eyeballs work good, so it's your job, okay? And if you keep on complaining—then me and Jeliza-Rose will cut off all your hair."

"Please don't," Magic Curl whimpered. "I'll behave."

"You better," I said. "You'd better just watch it."

In the bathroom, I left Magic Curl in front of the hatch.

"Please be careful," she said.

"We will," I replied.

"If we're not back in an hour," Classique told Magic Curl, "then come after us because it means we're being pulverized."

Then Classique and I crossed through the hatchway, where we soon found ourselves standing among the exposed fiberglass insulation of the farmhouse attic.

"It's a little cave," I said, blinking while my sight adjusted.

With daylight slanting in from a side vent, the attic was less dim than it had seemed.

Plumbing curved out of the wall behind us.

Electrical wiring, red and black and yellow, ran overhead.

Before us sat three cardboard boxes and a large trunk.

"Those boxes," Classique said, "let's take a look."

"I don't know."

"Are you scared again?"

"I don't know."

"Don't be. What's so spooky about a box?"

"It's the treasure chest that's spooky."

"But I bet there's only slippers and maybe gold in it."

"Or a killed thing," I said, thrusting Classique ahead as we ducked spiderwebs and a length of insulation that drooped from the sloped ceiling.

"It's Grandmother's stuff," said Classique.

"Yeah," I said, brushing a fine layer of dust off the cardboard tops.

All three boxes had been written on with a marker, each with a different word (LPs. PICTURE BOOKS. CHRIST-MAS). In the first box were old 78s, haphazardly packed, the plain wrappers just a bit more brittle than the records. The second box contained six photo albums, but we didn't recognize any of the faces in the black-and-white shots—children riding a scooter and a tricycle and a horse, men and women at a picnic in a field, a fishing trip, a wedding, an oblong brick home surrounded by other oblong brick homes.

"Strangers," Classique said. "Nobodies."

The third box offered broken Christmas ornaments, shattered in shards of green, silver, and red, with the hook attachments still intact.

"Worthless junk."

"Totally worthless. We need gold—and slippers. Gold slippers are good too."

The chest reeked of mothballs. Inside were three blond wigs, all tangled in a clump, which frightened me.

"It's a head." I said, stepping backwards.

"No," said Classique. "See, there's clothes."

I looked again, realizing the wigs belonged to a larger design: two long fluffy boas stretched alongside a baggy chemise. And there were hats. A bonnet, a pillbox, and a torn cloche. Deeper in the chest, sandwiched between the wraparounds and embroidered quilts, was a large mason jar containing a black cosmetic bag—as if the items within the bag were meant to be preserved forever, sealed away from the heat and dusty air of the attic.

"She wanted to be beautiful," I told Classique, picturing Grandmother at the front door of What Rocks, one of the boas wound about her neck, fluttering a gloved hand at someone; her crimson lips pursed, her blond wig styled and capped by the cloche.

"She wasn't beautiful," Classique said. "She was old."

"She was my grandmother."

"She was ugly with boxes of junk."

"You're lying," I said. "If you don't shut up, we're leaving."

But we stayed in the attic until I remembered Magic Curl. Then I turned and gazed at the hatchway. Classique nodded on my fingertip, but we didn't move. From our perspective, the hatch seemed almost as tiny as the knothole.

"We're squirrels," I finally said. "That's what we are."

But Classique couldn't say anything. I didn't want her to.

"Jeliza-Rose and Classique are outside looking for us," I said. "But they can't find where we're hiding."

And as we headed toward the bathroom, I removed her from my finger, clutched her in a fist, and pretended my footsteps left pawprints on the dirty floorboards.

7

I was planning on visiting the grazing pasture at dusk, where I'd wait in the bus for the fireflies. And I wouldn't let the train catch me off guard. That's why I dug Grandmother's cloth bonnet from the attic chest—when the train approached that evening, the bonnet would be on, tied securely under my chin, shielding my ears.

But after retrieving the bonnet, my shins began itching; I'd brushed against fiberglass as I crawled through the hatchway.

"It's awful," I told Classique in my bedroom.

"You'll make yourself bleed," she said, watching from my finger as I scratched at my shins. "Do it any harder and you'll cut yourself."

I kept scraping like mad until the pain became greater than the itchiness. Then I sighed with relief and flopped onto my bed.

"That's good," I said, my shins burning. "That's better."

"I'm bored. This is boring. Let's spin on the porch."

Classique hovered in front of my face like a fly, so I twirled my finger, rotating her in a circular motion.

"Stop it," she said. "I'll get dizzy and barf."

"No you won't. You can't. Your mouth doesn't work." I quit jiggling my finger, just in case.

My mother warned me about spinning in circles, not to do it in the apartment, especially following a meal. She said gyrating caused vomiting. But I never got sick. I spun during commercial breaks, arms outstretched. And I loved doing it in the living room—the carpet scrunching and the TV whizzing by—while my mother was unconscious, and my father slept on the couch. The wall pictures turned blurry with streaking colors and the shag carpet burned underfoot and snagged between my toes and the TV shot past as an eruption of static. Overhead, the bumpy ceiling swirled like a milk-white whirlpool and the plaster bumps were smoothed as the spinning increased, flattening everything, the edges all dissolved. Another spin in the opposite direction, the shag roots tugging and gritting, the living room easily shifting gears.

When my mother was awake, she could hear the sounds of my twirling from her bedroom. And she'd yell; I was only allowed to do splits in the living room, and handstands on my bed. The mattress was close to the floor, firm and wide. My neck wouldn't get broken if I fell. Still, handstands were tedious, so I usually did a couple before quitting. The splits were okay. Sometimes she had me do them in her bedroom, smiling as I brought my nose to the carpet. But spinning in the living room was what I loved, and the dizziness afterwards.

And on the farmhouse porch, I spun with itchy ankles, the wood slats groaning. It was the first time since leaving the apartment, though I considered having a whirl in the aisle of the Greyhound. With Classique and Magic Curl and Fashion Jeans on my fingertips, we went round and round, all four of us. Cut 'N Style stayed upstairs. She was just too blind.

"Eyes that can't see don't enjoy twirling," Classique concluded when I began gathering the heads. We never played with Cut 'N Style anyway, unless we had a tea party—then she became the guest of honor.

Our corner of the front porch was shaded. It felt cool and pleasant. Sunlight shined further on, landing across the steps leading to the yard. But our corner had fallen under siege: army ants traveled in three long lines, back and forth along the slats, up and down the newels. They came and went from the thin crack beneath the front door, carrying crumbs in their pincers; some had dust balls or what looked like bits of straw. I suspected that if one of the Barbies dropped in their midst, she'd quickly be hoisted and dumped off the porch, disappearing forever in the overgrowth below. So I spun in defense, performing pirouettes on the ants. Then I stomped all three ant lines, squashing the invaders, scrambling their ranks, chanting, "Save Cut 'N Style from the monsters! Save Cut 'N Style from the monsters!"

Cut 'N Style was unprotected on my pillow, surrounded by the torso, dismembered arms and legs. At Kmart, I once studied a brand new Cut 'N Style in her box. With hoop ear-rings, hands poised for clapping, red hair hanging to her butt, she was a stunning doll. Her baby-blue eyes glowed, and her Astronaut Fashion dress with matching go-go boots was an inspired touch. Years ago, my Cut 'N Style's head had been even more stylish than Classique–and that's why Classique hated her. In an effort to clean the black ink from Cut 'N Style's forehead and eyes, I poured nail polish remover over her face, just a few drops. But it smeared the red paint on her lips, blemished her plastic cheeks, and didn't put a dent in the ink.

"Now she's a complete freak," Classique said. "Get rid of her."

"I can't," I said. "What if it happened to you?"

"Then you should kill me."

The lines re-formed. The slats were overrun again.

For every crushed ant, at least two more arrived and began picking at the remains, the splat, the parts that hadn't been mashed into nothing. I was too dizzy to continue spin-ning, so I leaned against a newel and followed the lines with my wobbly vision. The army ants looked enormous and ancient, like runty dirt dobbers–except they didn't have wings.

On the soles of my sneakers, when I checked for bug parts, there were wet stains, dark and fresh, not unlike the chewing tobacco juice my father sometimes spit into a Coke bottle. And there was an ant head squirming in a tread, pincers still moving; the mangled body somewhere on the porch, or between the pincers of some other ant.

"Help me," it was trying to say. "I don't want to die. No, please–"

I brought my sneaker down, grinding the sole, then pounded it on the slats, making certain that the ant head was atomized.

"No mercy."

I singled out the biggest ants. I smushed their rear sections, allowing the front and middle sections to scramble away. Or I leveled the heads so only the rear and middle parts continued moving.

Then I watched.

The separated rear sections went astray, often slipping between the slats. But the head sections dragged themselves forward, showing no pain. So I picked them from the line and flicked them past the edge of the porch. To serve as a warning for the others, I didn't bother the rear parts. Sometimes a dumb ant explored one of the cleaved sections, but it couldn't understand what had happened. So it clambered on without a worry. But it didn't matter. I was tired of killing. These ants lacked intelligence anyway; they couldn't care any less about getting stomped–they weren't even interested in revenge. Squirrels were different. A squirrel would squish a person if given the opportunity.

"What do we do?" asked Classique.

Tugging Magic Curl and Fashion Jeans from my fingers, I said, "Wait, I got an idea."

Now I had a mission. So did Classique. Fashion Jeans and Magic Curl were hostages held by guerrilla forces; their heads sat on nail butts and the army ants roamed nearby. It was a desperate situation. But we could free only one, otherwise we might get noticed. Fashion Jeans was the obvious choice. She wasn't a whiney ass, so we'd save her.

I leapt across the porch, clearing enemy lines. Classique swooped down, almost sliding from my fingertip, and rescued Fashion Jeans before an ant reached her neck. But the mission hadn't been completed. We needed to get back. I sprinted over the ants–swinging my arms–and Classique went sailing. And when I picked her up from the porch, she said, "It's a stupid game. Let's do something else."

So we abandoned Fashion Jeans, and went searching for squirrels. But while skipping to the steps, I tripped. It was a mess. I tried getting hold of the railing, except I was stumbling and couldn't manage. My tailbone hit the top step; I sprang up. Then I fell. I couldn't stop myself, I was going too fast. My legs, my hands, elbows–they went crazy. I landed crosswise on the bottom step, clutching Classique. And for a moment I remained crumpled by the yard, like a monstrous foot had squashed me there. When I stood, splinters poked from the redness of my shins, thin slivers of wood sticking under the skin. I yanked them and then scratched. The itching was beginning again.

"I could've mashed you," I told Classique. "I could've fallen on you and you'd be dead."

Like that woman in Poland: she became suicidal after her husband said he was leaving. He told her that he was going to live with another woman. Then he left their apartment, which was on the tenth floor of a building. While he was exiting the lobby, his wife jumped from the balcony. She soared downward, hoping to collide with the sidewalk, and dropped smack-dab on her wanton husband's skull. Killing him. And she survived. I heard all about it during this TV show. Stranger Than Fiction, Amazing Stories of Life and Death. But my mother thought I was lying.

"A man tumbled into a coleslaw blender and got mixed to death."

"No he didn't."

"And another man tumbled into melted chocolate and died, and it happened to another man but it was gravy instead of chocolate. They died in vats."

"Jeliza-Rose, your stories aren't interesting."

"Do you know what this woman in New Zealand was stabbed to death with?"

"I don't care. That's enough."

"A frozen sausage. Can you believe it? And this man was in a coffin—"

"Enough. Seal it!"

But my father believed me. And when I explained about the workmen in Houston who tried freeing a squirrel from an irrigation pipe, he listened carefully.

"They lifted the pipe and it bumped a power wire, and they got zapped dead. But the squirrel was okay."

"Horrible," he said. "That's really awful."

And that second day at What Rocks, I spied a ghost lady near the railroad tracks, and wondered if she'd died horribly— if something like a frozen yogurt machine had electrocuted her, or a vat of molten lipstick was accidentally spilled on her. Or maybe she was lured to a wedding and murdered.

I wouldn't have seen the ghost if Classique hadn't asked to visit the bus. We'd been among the weeds, creeping around the farmhouse yard in hopes of spotting another squirrel, when she said, "Jeliza-Rose, show me that upside-down place."

"Okay," I told her, "but only you and me can go, and you can't tell anyone else because it's secret."

Then we snuck away toward the Johnsongrass, careful not to arouse Magic Curl and Fashion Jeans; their hollow necks stuck over nail butts on the front porch, hostages once more.

Stepping along the cattle trail, Classique and I quietly sang, "I'm a little tea pot, short and stout—" And as we reached the grazing pasture, I mentioned how the fireflies had materialized from nowhere.

"So now we can't sing or talk now," I said, dropping my voice, "or we'll spook the lightning bugs and they won't come tonight."

And when she said, "We must see the light bugs tonight," I put her against my lips and shushed her.

"You'll scare them," I said. "They probably won't be out tonight anyway."

I didn't want her returning with me that evening. The fireflies were my extra secret friends. Classique wouldn't understand their blinks.

Minding the bluebonnets that lurked in the high foxtails, we walked the length of the wreck. Then I bowed at a busted window, where the foxtail spikes tickled my chin. In midday, the upturned bus was smaller, less ominous than I remembered. And gazing straight through the gloomy interior, I caught sight of the Johnsongrass parting in the adjacent field— the ghost moving out into pasture, partially obscured by the rise of railroad tracks.

"It's a lady," I said, noting her black dress.

Her head was covered by a mesh hood, the kind beekeepers use for protection; she stooped—she didn't notice us. And the idea of running never crossed my mind. My heart didn't beat any faster, my hands didn't shake.

For a better view, Classique and I crept to the rear of the bus, my steps swooshing in the foxtails. And peeping around the side, we saw the ghost grabbing nettles, effortlessly, like pulling one Kleenex and then another from the box.

Ghost, I thought. Big fat ghost.

With the hood on, her housedress bunching as she crouched, the ghost appeared larger than any woman I'd ever encountered, including my mother. And while observing her at work, Classique and I were all whispers.

"She comes from a cave somewhere in that field," I said.

"Because she was killed in this very bus," said Classique, "all burned bad and that's why her face is covered."

"She boils what she pulls in a pot and makes weed soup. That's what she does."

"That's how ghosts get fat. There's so many weeds it'd be easy to get fat that way."

No other explanation presented itself.

On Halloween, I asked my father if ghosts haunted L.A., and he said just a few, mostly dead movie stars, like Marilyn Monroe and Fatty Arbuckle.

"But in Texas," he explained, "there's a ton. Bluesmen like Lightnin' Hopkins and Leadbelly wander Dallas streets at night. Woody Guthrie too. Then there's the Alamo–that joint is rich with spooks. And where Mother lived, way out in nowhere, she'd spot ghosts coming and going right outside her windows, right in the middle of the day."

"Bullshit," my mother said. "Noah, you'll be up with her tonight when she's scared to sleep."

"No I won't," my father told her, "'cause I'm saying now that most spooks are harmless. They just want to be seen but don't want to be bothered." Then he gave me one of his winks, saying, "As long as Mother was alive, them ghosts didn't bug her. In fact, she enjoyed knowing they was there. They kept an eye on her place, made her feel all safe."

And I was going to tell Classique what my father had said, but then my ankles were itching again, and my legs felt like needles were pricking at the skin but not quite sinking in.

"She got killed in the fire," whispered Classique.

Wrenching nettles from the ground and throwing them aside, the ghost paused to wipe dirt on her white apron. And even though it was warm outside, she wore gray mittens.

"No, she didn't get burned in the bus," I said. "She got strangled."

"And drowned."

"She's Queen Gunhild and she didn't want to stay in the bog so she decided not to be dead anymore."

Bog men rose from their peat graves, so did Gunhild. After all, she was a bog woman. And perhaps my father had become a ghost. He could be in the kitchen eating crackers, or upstairs searching for that squirrel. He might be on the porch, waiting.

"We have to go."

"Right now."

"We have to hurry."

But I couldn't run because my shins were sore. So we took our time.

The ghost was busy with her mittens, whistling a pretty song. The railroad tracks and the foxtails made it impossible to see what exactly her mittens were doing.

"He won't be on the porch," Classique said. "He won't be upstairs. He's not a ghost yet."

"But he will be."

"I know," she said. "I know everything."

I looked at her face, her long eyelashes. I wondered who removed her head. I wondered who did that kind of thing to dolls.

8

Classique said, "Quit scratching and it'll stop itching."

That's what my mother would tell me when I pinched at a scab or rubbed a bug bite.

"Just let it be and it'll heal quicker. You're making it worse."

So upstairs in the bathroom, I resisted the urge to rake my shins with my fingernails. Instead, I donned one of Grandmother's blond wigs. And standing at the mirror, I put on lipstick, trying my best to apply it evenly. If the lipstick ended up crooked or smeared, then it became poisonous. My tongue would swell, and I'd choke.

Grandmother's cosmetic bag had six different lipsticks, various shades of red, the scarlet being my favorite because it reminded me of apples. It also reminded me of blood. And it felt waxy like an apple peel but didn't dry like blood. I wondered if each lipstick had its own flavor and smell. I wondered if scarlet tasted good. I'd know when I finished; I'd bring the stick to my tongue and lick it. Then I could slide it between my lips–I'd study my reflection, how the stick went in and out–and see what flavor it had. I could bite into the stick if I wanted; I could chew it in my mouth like gum. But that was too risky. I didn't want my tongue swelling—microscopic syringes hid in the lipstick.

I spread it carefully. If I went any quicker my hand might get shaky and the lipstick would end up all over my chin; it might redden my nose. Then the poison would be released. A gradual application was the safest bet, stay within the borders, no hurry—like drawing in my Barbie Coloring Book. It was easy coloring the dresses or hair. But the heads and arms and legs were difficult to get right; they were so thin, my crayons always scooted past the borders if I hurried. When I wasn't meticulous, the picture got ruined, and Barbie had to be ripped from the pages. And I cursed myself.

Careful. Almost done. Deadly lips as delicious as an apple. Dream Date Jeliza-Rose doll. When the lipstick reached the nooks of my mouth I had to pause; it was hard getting the scarlet neatly in the corners.

My reflection glowered. She suddenly resembled my mother and it frightened me. She said, "Get on with it. You little bitch, I'm hungry." She was staring into my eyes, gazing through me.

I glanced down. The lipstick moved. I felt it smear and looked up. The scarlet had smudged across my upper lip, daubed between my nostrils. Doomed. My reflection smiled with her crazy wig and messy lips. Murderer. I'd been poisoned.

Grasping my throat, I ran into my bedroom.

"Classique, I'm dying. My tongue is filling my head. I can't talk anymore because I'm really dying now."

"Dear, you're already dead," she told me. "You're a ghost!"

"Already?"

"A spook."

I touched the blond coils hanging on my forehead.

"And so beautiful too. I'm a vision."

"Very beautiful," she said. "More beautiful than—I don't know."

"More beautiful than—"

Scampering, rapid light-sounding steps came from behind. I turned. I couldn't believe it.

The squirrel was at the bathroom door, puffy tail curled– he sniffed the floor; I watched him. That twitching muzzle. He was almost motionless, hunched in the doorway. I wondered what to do, but I couldn't think–I could only watch. It was as if he didn't see me, and I wasn't afraid of him. I just didn't know what to do.

Then he cocked his head to one side, considering me. His paws flexed on the floorboards. I waited to see if he seemed fearful; then I worried that other squirrels were coming, a hit squad. When I took a deep breath, he swung around, facing me, went up on his hind legs, sniffing. He wasn't scared.

"What do you want? How'd you get in?"

I knew the squirrel was fast. And he was mean. He could spring through the air. He might bite me. He might steal Classique, eat her hair, and gnaw her into nothing with those nasty teeth. It was creepy, an animal always chewing on wood or wires or plastic things. He did it because he was a pig and couldn't hunt food like a lion. He was also stupid. But his teeth were huge, tusks, worse than claws. While attacking, he could sink into a skull as easy as someone crunching into an apple.

"You better leave," I said, a warning for good measure, but it didn't rattle him. "You go!"

His tail swooshed. He couldn't quit sniffing. His ears quivered.

I threw the wig at him. But it missed; he was already scrambling, tearing through the room.

So I hurdled onto my bed, screaming, "Go away!"

The squirrel was confused and chirping like a bird; his knothole was somewhere else. He sprang from one end of the room to the other, desperate for a good climbing place–a wall without a ceiling overhead, just sky. Back and forth across the throw rug. Chattering and angry. That was the worst part. Squirrel babble near my bed and me and the dolls. Then under the bed, then out, across the throw rug again, to the wall–to the other wall. Hesitate, sniff, stand, down, run. Chatter, chirp. Back under the bed, out. Across the throw rug. Wall to wall.

I hobbled on the mattress, yelling, bouncing the doll parts. Doll heads leaping. Some of them mashed by my feet, like ants. Toes on Classique, toes on Fashion Jeans. Jumping and shouting.

Then he froze, no good climbing place, no knothole. I couldn't scream anymore; the breath had abandoned me. My shins were itching. The wig sat in a clump. The room smelled like skunk.

"Just go–"

He shot into the bathroom, skidding on the floor. Claws scratching; he was frantic, irate. Hopping about in there, making a racket–then he was gone.

"You don't come back!" I yelled, stepping to the floor.

But I knew he wouldn't return; that was why I left the bed. I was going to discover how he got inside What Rocks; it didn't make sense. I stood at the bathroom doorway. I glanced over a shoulder, like a paratrooper on the verge of plunging. I was alone. Classique and the others had been bounced into unconsciousness. They probably wouldn't join me anyway, not on this mission. So I entered the bathroom, tip-toeing, with eyes alert and ready.

I noticed the hatch at once; it was slightly open, wide enough for a squirrel. When I brought the wig and cosmetic bag from the attic, I'd forgotten to shut the night latch. And peeking through the opening I spotted him. He was near the chest. He was nibbling on scrap wood, holding it in his paws. I didn't yell or call for Classique. I didn't want the squirrel to know I'd found him. This was how it should be–me spying on him while he did squirrel stuff, like nibble and then clean his face by wetting his paws. I wasn't mad that the squirrel got in the attic. This was better than stalking him outside.

Also, I liked the idea of doing something without Classique, but she often became jealous if I ignored her. So I'd make certain she wouldn't know about the squirrel, how I could see his busy paws, his head between them as he rubbed at his snout, cleaning. I could see him scratching his side with a hind leg. I was thrilled. I could have clapped my hands with delight. But I was scared to make a sound, or everything might get ruined.

I could hear Classique stirring, whispering my name. But I didn't answer. I'd wait by the hatch until the squirrel went away, then I'd leave the bathroom before Classique panicked. But she kept saying my name; she'd whisper it all day, thinking the squirrel had punctured my brain and dragged me into the attic for a chew.

I wanted to scratch my shins. It was humid here, heat pushing from the attic. It was hot. The squirrel sniffed and glanced my way.

Caught.

He bit the air with his teeth. He tried to bluster me, to bully my eyes, to keep me from looking.

We were gazing at each other now, waiting for one another to bolt. It'd be finished soon; Classique would know I was in the bathroom and bellow. These were the final seconds of just me and the squirrel. Next thing, he was scampering toward the vent. He was squeezing between the slants, gone again.

"The wig needs help! It's in trouble! Where are you?"

It was Classique.

"Don't rush me," I said, pushing the night latch. "I'm in here minding my own business."

And as I exited the bathroom, my right foot landed on the wig and I almost slipped.

"See there," said Classique. "That wig is trouble."

"That's not what you said," I told her.

"That's exactly what I said."

I put the wig on. Then Classique.

"I'm hungry," I said. "Are you?"

"Silly," she said, "I don't have a stomach. It goes in my mouth and drops on the floor like pooh."

"Gross." I laughed. "You're gross. Now I'm not hungry."

But I was lying; nothing could prevent me from eating. Not even army ants. They were in the kitchen, raiding the saltines. They crawled around the rim of the peanut butter jar, explored the water jug. They'd stolen chunks from a Wonder Bread slice. It bothered me. But I should've sealed everything up the night before. Then all the ants could scavenge were crumbs, and the peanut butter smeared on the counter–I'd been sloppy–and the bread crust I'd removed like a scab, tossing it aside. They were welcome to the crust. I hated it more than them.

So I ate without destroying any ants. I just thumped them from the jar, from the cracker box.

"Pulverize them," said Classique. "Make them die."

She was annoyed. She was pouting. She'd got peanut butter in her hair when I'd scooped some with a finger. I was always getting junk in her hair, glue or toothpaste. She worried her hair would fall out. Aside from her rooted eyelashes, it was all she had, and she had lots of it–but baldness still tormented her. I was concerned too, so at home I bathed her and washed her hair. I never used a lot of shampoo and I always combed it afterwards. Every time. Her red hair was thick. If I didn't comb it, she'd go frizzy and look stupid.

"These ants are evil," said Classique. "They're poisoning everything. It isn't funny."

"But it's my fault." I'd finished my peanut butter crackers and was licking my finger-knife. "They'd go somewhere else if I didn't make messes."

It was dumb, not putting the food away. Bread slices left out overnight were hard and withering; I sprinkled water on them but it didn't help. Now I was going to have to let the ants finish them. Dozens of pincers clamping and ripping. Piranhas. They'd get so fat they'd pop.

Wonder Bread bombs, I thought. Ants exploding on the porch.

Serves them right, thought Classique.

We could suddenly read each other's minds. We were psychic. Like those people on TV.

In the 1500's, Nostradamus predicted the rise of Hitler and the assassination of John F. Kennedy. He was a physician and an astrologer. He was also French. The Loch Ness monster, via extrasensory perception, communicated with an elderly Scottish woman every Friday. She refused to say what it told her. The Bible foretold the disaster in Chernobyl. Dion Warwick relied on psychic friends for picking her hit singles. Ghosts appreciated receiving gifts, like cookies or toys; it was a way of acknowledging their presence, of befriending them. Six out of ten twins could read each other's minds. It was all true. It was on TV.

The ghost is sending us a message.

What is it?

I'm not sure.

If we go upstairs we can see her, I think.

We can look out the window and see her.

Yes. Come on—

We raced upstairs, vaulting every other step. And going to my bedroom window, short of breath, we looked hopefully for the ghost—but even if she was haunting the field, the Johnsongrass and bus blocked our view.

I sighed. There were moth bodies outside, near the window ledge, dotting the roof. I didn't feel like being psychic anymore; my brain hurt.

"I don't see her."

"She wanted something. Ghosts appreciate gifts."

I nodded and sucked the peanut butter from Classique's hair. Then I asked, "What can we give her?"

"Not just anything," she told me. "It's got to be useful. A good gift."

"Like cookies."

"Except we don't have cookies anyway."

I would have killed for some cookies, Oreos or Nutter Butters. I loved them almost as much as Crunch bars.

"It doesn't need to be food," she said.

"I could draw a picture of you and me."

"Or give her Cut 'N Style."

"Or Magic Curl."

I imagined Magic Curl squirming in the ghost's palm and blubbering like a baby; she'd wet herself, if she could.

"Something else."

There was lipstick on Classique's hair. I closed my eyes. On TV, a little boy in Germany shut his eyes and foresaw the future. He predicted that dark clouds would gather above his village and rain toads. The next day, after a violent thunderstorm, thousands of dying toads flopped on the village streets.

"What can only a dead person use?" she said. "Think."

"I can't think. Crackers?"

"Or the radio. It's dead too."

I opened my eyes. "Yes. She can listen to ghost voices then."

"And ghost music."

"But Daddy likes it."

"He's not a ghost yet. He doesn't need it."

"That's right. I forgot."

In the living room, I reached for the radio without glimpsing my father's face. I lifted it from his lap. I knew he was staring behind the sunglasses. And as Classique and I ran outside, I fiddled with the dial. I listened; no music, no static. KVRP, eclectic music for eclectic minds. That was the station I wanted. But it wouldn't come in. I couldn't hear anything, where one station ended and another began.

"It's the perfect gift," I concluded. "It really is."

"I think so too."

The ghost was nowhere to be seen, so we struggled through the high weeds, up the rise, across the railroad tracks, but not before I made certain a train wasn't approaching. Then we slinked down the embankment, and crept into the field—a portion of which had been cleared, the earth brown and bumpy from uprooting. Pulled nettles were discarded in a pile.

"She's not making soup."

"Not even for potions."

She'd trampled foxtails to the ground, yanked and tossed nettles. She'd stacked stones and rocks—just to save bluebonnets. That's what her mittens had been tending. The field was littered with the spring flowers, and the ghost was protecting them.

"She doesn't like us here," Classique said. "Be quick."

So I set the radio on the ground and began encircling it with the biggest of the stacked rocks, careful not to disturb any flowers. I told myself that the ghost would welcome the courtesy, but I wasn't sure. After all, I was returning rocks to the field, creating a jagged circle among her flowers.

"That's good."

"Let's go."

As we clamored up the embankment, Classique sent me a thought–she'll know what to do with the radio.

I saw it on TV. A man in New Mexico could turn his radio dial and tune in the raspy voices of deceased loved ones. Sometimes his television broadcast his dead son playing soccer in a foggy meadow; he had proof, he had a videotape.

Of course, I thought. She'll understand. She's a ghost.

And moving over the tracks, we heard the quarry boom, a faint explosion, like a distant thunderclap.

"It's magic," I said, gazing at the clear sky. "They're making thunder. That's what they do."

9

I hypnotized myself by swinging a Barbie arm in front of my face.

I said, "Your legs won't itch anymore. And you won't scratch them for four years."

Then I hypnotized Classique and the others.

"You are sleepy," I told them. "You are so sleepy and you are sleeping. You are dreaming of trains, of Eskimo Pies and old men dancing with bears. Cut 'N Style, my voice is knocking you out. And you too Fashion Jeans. And Magic Curl. Classique, you're sleeping. You won't wake up until I say. You won't know where I'm going, ever." The arm worked like a charm.

They were snoring. They were snuggled on the blond wig.

I stepped backwards from the room, watching them, thinking—sleep, sleep, little dear ones, sleep. Then I turned and went downstairs.

Now it was almost dusk. I sat in the bus, on the ceiling, wearing the bonnet. Everything smelled of smoke, even my dress. A breeze roamed all around, blowing away some of the humidity; the air had become cooler. I looked for fireflies.

But it wasn't quite time. The sun still poked above the Johnsongrass. And the light inside the bus was slowly shifting, the sharp edges of the broken windows shimmered—the springs, fluff, and burnt upholstery on the overhead seats radiated, orange and white.

Someone had carved into the metal wall, a corroded scrawl I hadn't noticed before. The words were upside-down—etched higher than I could reach—but easy to read: LOIS YOU SUCK BUTT!

"Suck butt," I said. "You suck butt." What a crazy thing to do. I didn't want to think about it. "That's dumb," I told myself.

When my father and I walked toward the L.A. River, we often stopped to read graffiti. Whole sides of buildings were decorated with slang, sprayed symbols and designs, red and blue and silver and black, like pictures from a comic book.

"It's all beautiful," my father said. "People hate it."

"What's it mean?"

"Names, mostly. Gang stuff. I'm not sure."

Framing an entire doorway was a Valentine's heart, full and perfect, pierced by a stiletto.

"You know what that is."

"Love," I said.

"Yep."

We'd come back to the same building a week later, but the graffiti wouldn't be there, just whitewashed patches hiding names and colors and massive hearts. It was gross. "They should leave it alone," I said.

"Don't worry, whitewash doesn't last long, not in this neighborhood."

There was a tunnel in the middle of Webster Park—cutting underneath a pathway—where bums slept and teenagers drank beer and smoked. Instead of crossing over the tunnel, my father and I usually strolled through it, dodging broken bottles and the occasional vagrant zipped up in a sleeping bag. And once we found a spray paint can. Silver Lustre. So my father shook the can, then painted a smiley face on the cement. "That's you," he said. "That's how you look today."

"No it's not. That's not me today."

"Well, it must be you tomorrow."

He handed me the can.

"Give it a try."

I was going to make a smiley face too, but I had the valve aimed wrong and sprayed my right hand.

"Oh no," I said, dropping the can.

There was wet Silver Lustre in my palm; I dabbed it off on my pink shirt. I wanted to cry, but my father was laughing. He was laughing so much he started coughing. I thought he was getting sick.

My mother was waiting when we arrived home. She saw my shirt first, two silver handprints where a pink pony and a balloon should be. "What the hell happened to you?" She grasped my wrists, flipping my hands.

"I'm a robot," I said.

Then she slapped me.

"You've ruined that shirt! Your hands!"

But the worst part was my father. He didn't do anything. He just stood by the front door and said nothing. And I wanted to yell at him for laughing in the tunnel. I wanted him to explain that it was all his fault, that it was his idea to play with the can.

MOM YOU SUCK BUTT! That's what I should've sprayed on the cement. That's what I should've told her after she slapped me.

I scanned the walls for more carvings, but the sun had dipped below the Johnsongrass, making my search difficult. So I gazed at the pasture, where a few fireflies were already flashing.

"I'm here," I shouted. "In here! It's me!"

Then I covered my mouth, shutting myself up. I'd been too loud. The ghost could've heard me. She might think I was calling her.

Glancing across the passageway, through the windows, I saw her meadow. But, because of the railroad tracks and weeds, I couldn't see the bluebonnets or the rocks encircling the radio. Or the ghost, if she was there. And beyond the meadow, glowing among a cluster of mesquite trees, was a yellow light, a thousand times the size of a firefly blink; the queen mother of all fireflies–I thought–lurking in the distance, at least a mile from me and the bus.

On the other side of the tracks, everything seemed bigger–the flowers, the rocks, the rows of Johnsongrass. And the ghost.

"She can destroy Tokyo like Godzilla," I'd told Classique. "She'd make Mom's bed go crash."

"She's Queen Gunhild. Queens are always fatter than everyone. That's how they become queens. Everyone gives her gold and food to eat and she gets fat and sits on scales in her court, so then everyone has to give her more food and gold–it has to be the same as how fat she is."

"Queens are monsters. They need to be strangled and drowned in bogs."

I imagined my mother in the meadow, killing nettles and hurling rocks. And she knew I was inside the bus. And she was hungry. Soon she'd climb over the rise and onto the tracks. She'd be coming after me: "You miserable creep!"

The fireflies were here, floating through the windows. They flashed everywhere, but I wasn't really paying attention. I looked back and forth, from one window to another, in case someone was sneaking outside. I tried sending psychic messages to Classique–wake up now, wake up, I'm in trouble–but she was dreaming of Eskimo Pies. I was on my own. And my father relaxed in Denmark. He wouldn't help even if my mother was choking me, even if she was ripping my head off.

So I waited.

When the train came I'd run. I was near the bus door, the escape exit. My father said a person could easily outrun a ghost or a bog man or any monster.

"They only get you when you aren't expecting them. If you're expecting them, you can always get away."

"But they're fast."

"No, they aren't fast. Dead things are slow. You have to be alive to run. Your heart has to be pumping."

"Why?"

"Because if your heart ain't pumping then you're dead. And if you're dead, you can't run."

"How do you move, if you're dead?"

"You don't. You just flutter, I guess. Like a leaf in the wind. Energy or something takes you from one place and puts you somewhere else. It's like magic. If your dead, you need a ton of magic—a lot more than a living person does."

I couldn't figure it. But I believed him anyway.

"So you run when you see a monster?"

"Or before you see it. When you sense it. When you know it's about to pop up and grab you. Not like in movies. People are always idiots in movies. They wait to get caught. They fall and look back and scream. Just run. Then you're safe."

No more waiting. The train was late. There were bog men in the sorghum; I heard them rustling. And Queen Gunhild wanted food. But I was alive, so I ran.

My sneakers mashed foxtails and bluebonnets. Sorry, I thought, sorry. I didn't look back or scream.

I just sent messages: Classique, hear me. You are awake and not sleeping anymore. You are awake and not sleeping anymore. You are awake—

Fireflies flashed on the cattle trail, so I kept my mouth closed. I didn't want to swallow one. If I swallowed one, my stomach might start blinking. Then if I had to hide in the tall weeds, it'd be a cinch seeing me; I'd be like Bugs Bunny, strolling in front of Elmer Fudd with a target pattern on his butt, saying, "Say, doc, what makes you think there's a rabbit in these woods?"

"Oh, I doughn't know. Just a wittle hunch."

Racing toward the front yard, I caught the sound of the train. The earth trembled with its passing. I paused beside the flag pole, panting, and felt the steel vibrate against my shoulder. The Johnsongrass trembled under the breeze, and goose bumps rose on my arms. There was no one following along the cattle trail, not yet. I tried peering through the rows of sorghum, but it was impossible. I knew what was happening though—in the grazing pasture, fireflies were being buffeted from the bus. Chunks of glass clattered in the burnt-out passageway, some fell like hail from the windows. And, for a while at least, Queen Gunhild couldn't cross the tracks.

Classique was communicating, a faint transmission: It's okay. I'm awake. Come get me—

Then no noise, no train, no breeze. My palms were sweating like crazy. But I was safe. I walked onto the porch and entered the house.

My father was in the chair. I could see the back of his head. And the map of Denmark was sagging, drooping over; a top corner had come unstuck. For a moment I considered fixing the map, but that meant getting close to him. He'd probably changed colors again, and the thought of his skin spooked me—especially now that the farmhouse had grown darker. He was like the Mood Ring in my mother's jewelry box; sometimes turning blue, sometimes black. That ring never worked right.

The dressing gown lay in the entryway, at the front door, so I picked it up. The satin was so soft. I pressed it against my cheek.

"Smooth as a baby's butt," I said, calmed by my own voice.

I have an idea, Classique was thinking.

What?

Come get me and I'll tell you.

I cradled the dressing gown like a baby. There wasn't a light for the stairs; it was pitchy, the steps were invisible. But I pretended a baby's butt rested in the nook of my arms, and that made me happy.

"I love you so much," I told the dressing gown. "You're my dear sweet one."

And when I showed Classique my baby, she said, "It's dead. It doesn't have bones."

She was the only one awake on the wig.

"I don't care. It's smooth."

"It doesn't have a pumping heart."

"But you don't too."

"How do you know?" she said. "I might."

"I'm sorry."

I didn't want to argue. She could be stubborn. If I argued with her, she wouldn't explain her idea—although I already understood what it was. So I gently laid the dressing gown on the pillow, then I slipped Classique onto my finger.

"Get the wig," she said.

I grabbed the wig, tumbling Fashion Jeans and Magic Curl and Cut 'N Style across the mattress. Then I went into the bathroom and got the cosmetic bag. And before going, I noticed that the hatch was ajar, beyond which existed murkiness, outer space, a void where the Bog Man could hibernate. The attic wasn't the same as in the daytime; it was another world, the black hole of What Rocks. I tried setting the latch, but the bolt wouldn't stay in its notch. I pressed hard with my palm. When I let off, the bolt sprang back. So I removed a tiny toothbrush from the bag—its bristles stained with mascara—and wedged the hilt in the gap between the hatch and the baseboard.

"You don't move," I ordered the brush, "or you'll die."

Sometimes toothbrushes died. The bristles dulled and that was that. Sneakers died too. And buildings. So did Moms and Dads. The planet was full of the dying, the dead, the gone. But if someone was beautiful, like Classique, they could go on forever. Death was ugly.

In the living room I whispered, "You're a vision."

The wig fit my father well, the blond coils almost concealed his ponytail.

"You're a sensation."

His face remained pallid. He hadn't changed much during the day. And I was relieved. There was a compact of rouge in the cosmetic bag—so I dabbed color on his cheeks, on his chin, on his earlobes, brightening the purple blotches. Then I removed the bonnet and put it on him.

He was pretty now. So I kissed his mouth. The skin felt fake and rubbery. I kissed him more than once, until the scarlet reddened his lips. Then I sat at his boots with Classique and admired him.

"We're very proud of you," I told him. "You're Miss America."

And that night I slept in his room with the door locked. Just me and Classique. For a while, from the window, I watched the tower strobe flicker. But I didn't stare too long. I didn't want to get hypnotized. Then I lay on his mattress, very quietly. I shut my eyes, transmitting messages downstairs.

Daddy—? This is me. Am I coming in loud and clear? Daddy—? If you can hear me, say something. It's me. Radio Jeliza-Rose, broadcasting from your bedroom. Are you there?

10

Sitting on the porch steps, I sipped from the gallon jug and then dribbled into Classique's hair. There wasn't any shampoo in What Rocks, so I pretended. I scrubbed her scalp like it was soapy. The water made her red hair look brown.

I called her Miss.

"How would you like it today, Miss?" And, "Miss, could I possibly interest you in some of our exclusive hair-care products?"

But she told me to just shampoo, to not talk.

"Yes, Miss."

The customer was always right, even when she was wrong. So I combed my fingers through Classique's hair, pushed at her plastic skull, and shut up. And if she was my mother, I'd be tapping my fist on her head, like knocking on a door–but softer. Then I'd uncoil my fist, letting my fingertips spread slowly out. It gave my mother the chills.

"Cracking an egg."

"Do me now."

We took turns. My mother and I. Cracking eggs on each other's heads. Often we rapped with both hands, two fists crumbling, and the fingertips would then drip all over, an oily feeling, trickling toward the neck, around the ears, the forehead. Gooseflesh. I loved that game.

Spider, Pinch, Blow–another chill game.

"Spider crawling up your spine–"

Fingertips creeping along the back to the shoulders.

"Tight squeeze–"

Pinching the shoulder blades.

"Cold breeze–"

Blowing on the neck while dragging nails down the spine.

"Now you've got the chills."

It never failed. The bumps grew, rough and pimply. I'd rub my arms and neck so they'd go away. "Do it again," I'd tell my mother, once the bumps disappeared. "Just one more."

"That's what you said before."

"But I promise. Just one more."

And sometimes we shampooed each other's hair. But we didn't use water or shampoo. We did it in her bedroom. It was all make-believe.

My mother always said, "Could I interest you in some of our exclusive hair-care products, miss?"

"No thank you," I replied. "Not today."

I wanted her to stroke my scalp without saying anything. I closed my eyes, knowing the massage wouldn't last long, wishing she'd never stop. She could've put me asleep, easily; I would've liked that.

But Classique wasn't growing sleepy. As I rinsed her hair, she was wide awake, gazing beyond the yard, studying the gray clouds that stretched overhead. The sun was hiding; I couldn't see where.

That morning, fog hugged the ground, obscuring everything. In my father's bedroom, I parted the curtains above the bed. "We're flying," I told Classique, imagining What Rocks adrift in some cloud. By the time I dressed and went outside with the jug, the fog had lifted. The farmhouse had descended through the grim sky, returning safely to

Grandmother's property.

Now I wrung Classique's hair, shaking the water from my hand, saying, "It'll lightning. It'll flood and What Rocks will float off with us."

Then, in order to prevent frizziness, I smoothed her hair between my palms.

"You're shiny," I told her. "You're cleaner than soap."

Classique ignored me. She was angry because I didn't use shampoo. She thought I was spitting in her hair. And spit stunk. I explained that the water came from the jug, that I was only dribbling so she wouldn't get too wet.

"What can I do?" I asked. "I'll help you get happy."

"Do you want to check the radio? If it's still there—"

"Do you?"

"Yes."

We were of the same mind.

I ran as fast as possible toward the railroad tracks, holding Classique aloft; that way her hair would dry quicker. When we climbed the rise, I crouched in the weeds by the tracks, but the ghost wasn't there. So I walked down into her meadow, which had an earthy, moist smell like after rain. Stormy clouds swirled over the sorghum and behind them a hazy sun, round as the moon, hiding out.

Classique and I went to where we left the gift.

"She's been here," I said, squatting by the rocks.

The radio was gone.

"She found it."

"And look what she did—"

The rocks were rearranged, spaced evenly, making a figure eight; in each loop a freshly planted bluebonnet. I saw it as a sign, an acknowledgment, a thank you. And a response was expected. So I set Classique in a loop, under a bluebonnet, and began shifting rocks. But I couldn't think what to do. Another circle was pointless. A square or an arrow seemed dumb.

A smiley face then.

"The universal mark of friendship," was how my father described smiley faces. "In Japan or Holland or Mexico, it always means the same thing." He never gave autographs, just smiley faces with his initials jotted underneath the grin.

In my Big Chief sketch book, my father and I sat for hours at the dining table, drawing pictures with crayons. I made sunflowers or Barbies or stick figures parachuting. And he colored black grins, black-dot eyes, black-dot noses, of various shapes and sizes—but unmistakable. He'd fill page after page with them. Once he made an American flag with nothing but red, white, and blue smiley faces.

Then there was the song he sometimes sang while tucking me in bed.

> Don t be wonderin if I love you
> Cause I m a lecherous so-and-so
> Just take a hard look at my face
> And my smile will let you know
> All you think you need to know

And I hummed that song as my hands upheaved the rocks. The ghost would find my universal sign of friendship, and she'd probably laugh or smile. She'd probably whistle her pretty tune, fully aware that someone cared about her. The next day, I planned on returning—then I could see what she created with the rocks.

But it didn't happen like that.

I should've noticed Classique because she was looking past me, too horrified to speak; her blue eyes were huge and unblinking. But I wasn't paying attention. I was busy working, pressing a rock into the soil with both hands.

The clouds parted. The sun suddenly shone behind me. A great shadow swept across my back and onto the half-finished rock grin—the ghost's broad silhouette, the beekeeper's hood cast at an angle. I froze; my heart almost burst from my chest, my hands trembled.

"Child," her low voice said, "what are you doing?" She sounded like a man, like my father in the morning, his throat gravelly and hoarse.

I couldn't answer. My legs couldn't run. My hands wouldn't stop shaking.

The shadow moved. I heard her footsteps clomping, coming toward me. From the corners of my eyes, I saw the hem of her housedress swish by, the muddy brown high boots she wore.

Then she stood in front of me, nudging at the rocks with a boot tip, saying, "This won't do, you know. You've ruined my cat eyes."

Cat eyes? Not a figure eight then. But cat eyes, with bluebonnets for pupils.

I raised my head slowly, scanning the length of her; the white apron, the gray mittens, the pith helmet draped on all sides by the hood. Her arms were crossed. I could see her features in the mesh—big nose, big jaw, gold-rimmed glasses.

Ghost, I thought, please leave. You're scaring me.

"Are you mute, vandal?" she asked. "You can't speak?"

I shook my head.

"What's that mean? No or yes?"

"I'm scared," I muttered.

"Vandal is scared," she said. "As you should be, I think."

She had me confused with someone else.

"I'm not Vandal," I told her.

"What?"

"I'm not Vandal. I'm Jeliza-Rose."

"What kind of rose?"

"Jeliza—"

"Uh-huh," she said, nodding. She repeated my name to herself, rolling it around in her mouth like a marble. Then she went, "Well, a vandal by any other name—do you understand?"

"No."

She unfolded her arms, saying, "It doesn't matter, I suppose."

Then she sighed, poking at the rocks again for a moment.

In the brooding sunlight, transfixed by the ghost, touching the ground with my fingertips, the fear that had seized me was now settling. I didn't need to runaway just yet; I could wait a little longer.

"Any bees?"

I managed a shrug.

"One sting and I'm paralyzed," she said. "One sting and I'm most likely dead."

"You're dead," I told her.

The ghost gasped as if I'd startled her. "What a thing to say," she said. "What kind of child are you?"

I shrugged.

"Well then, if you see a bee–or hear a bee–you'll say so, right?"

I nodded.

"If I'm stung and die, it'll be your fault."

Her mittens were at the hood, turning up the mesh, bringing the net-like fabric over the helmet. The hair hanging on her forehead seemed unnaturally yellow, recalling the discolored corners of the brittle newspaper my father kept in his closet–KING OF ROCK 'N' ROLL DEAD.

A ghost's face?

Nope, thought Classique.

But she was white. She had a pinkish color, a jowly, abstracted appearance–a weathered countenance that was also unforgiving, wrinkled, graceful. Her glasses lacked a left lens, the right lens was shaded and impenetrable.

"They'll stay far," she was saying to herself, drawing a circle in the air. "They'll mess elsewhere."

I wasn't sure if she was referring to me and Classique, or the bees.

She clapped her hands together, once. She pivoted her head and spit. "That'll keep them gone for a bit," she told me. "It usually works. You'd be surprised."

Then she knelt, scrutinizing the disrepair at her feet. And like a parachute sinking to the earth, the hem of her housedress billowed and ruffled outward. She reached for the rocks I'd rearranged–shaking her head some–and began fixing her cat eyes.

"See, everything has a place," she said, moving the rocks. "Even the smallest thing. If you tamper with something–take it from its place—there's no order. And then there's no light. Everything is chaos."

She paused and regarded Classique sitting under the bluebonnet.

"And is this for me?"

"It's Classique. She's my friend."

She extracted Classique, pinching her between a forefinger and thumb, thrusting her out and away like a stinky sock.

"You should consider the company you keep, I think. Take it."

I leaned forward, gingerly accepting Classique. And I watched as the mittens patted dirt, adjusted the stems of the bluebonnet-pupils, hoisted rocks.

"Can I help you?"

"Certainly not. In fact, you'll be going. I've nothing more to say. You've blinded a cat eye."

"But I can help."

"Uh-huh, well, go and help me. Go, I mean. That'll help me. You belong somewhere else."

She squinted—one eye showing, the other concealed behind that dark lens—reminding me of a pirate. Then she grabbed the mesh, pulling it past her face, a door slamming shut.

It wasn't fair; I could help with her garden. And now she was ignoring me. "You're not a real ghost," I said, standing.

"I should think not—not yet."

Rotten old woman, I thought.

And I regretted giving her the radio. She didn't thank me—and she was mean to Classique. So I left her. I turned and ran. But as I climbed the rise, she called after me.

"Rose-Jeliza," she said, "what else can you do?"

I played deaf. And scrambling onto the tracks, I stood upright, frowning, and gazed back down into the meadow. She was dusting the mittens on her apron, giving me a sideways glance.

"Child, what is it you like to do," she pointed at the cat eyes, "besides messing with this?"

I couldn't think, so I said what sprang first to mind: "I fight squirrels–and I eat too."

She was quiet for a while. She scratched her chin through the mesh.

"Very well," she finally said. "If you come here around noon tomorrow we'll eat, how's that? But go now, go to where you came from, where you belong. I've nothing more to say. Just come tomorrow then–and forget your friend, she's trouble."

My frown straightened. "Okay," I said.

And heading toward the farmhouse, I forced a laugh, a cackle. I threw Classique in the air and caught her. If the ghost wasn't really a ghost, at least she was friendly, almost. And tomorrow we'd eat together, maybe even crack eggs on each other.

But Classique was miserable. She sulked all the way home.

"She doesn't hate you," I reassured her. "She doesn't."

But Classique didn't care what I had to say to her. And neither did I. She was trouble, after all.

Two

11

Classique, let me tell you about the picnic with the ghost, and what I saw and did afterwards. I'm so sorry you couldn't go because the food was wonderful, better than crackers and peanut butter; she brought a tasty treat–dark greasy meat like on a chicken thigh (I'm not sure that's what it was though), served on a linen napkin that had lacy patterns. And apple juice. And pound cake, half a slice. I didn't eat that much, but I still ate enough to make me sleepy.

But let me tell you first how I waited for the ghost.

Of course, she isn't a ghost. You knew that. Her name is Dell, and she lives in the far-off mesquite cluster, in a small home made of gray and russet-colored stone. I followed her after our picnic, but she didn't know. At least I don't think she did.

But before, in her meadow, I sat cross-legged by the cat eyes for at least an hour. The sky was clear, the air breezy. The Johnsongrass murmured from time to time, as if someone was wandering among the sorghum–but it was only the wind tricking me. And, as you know, I wore lipstick and rouge. My hands were clean (I'd washed up on the porch, using the gallon jug, splashing water into a cupped palm. Then I worked my front teeth under the crest of each finger-nail, scraping out the dirt).

And just when I thought Dell had forgotten me, she pushed through the Johnsongrass, saying half my name. "Rose, Rose, Rose—"

She held a wicker picnic basket in one hand, carried a quilt in the other.

From behind the hood she said, "Have you been here long? I should think not, no. You haven't touched my cat eyes. You haven't ruined a thing. You've been here minutes, I suppose."

That throaty man's voice, that froggy grumble.

"Hurry, child. We're burning sunshine and I don't have all day."

Then she was leaving the way she came, marching off in the sorghum, receding, so I jumped to my feet and went after her, skipping.

Soon I was traveling in new territory, going away from What Rocks and the tracks. And Dell was asking, "Were you born of coyotes? Are you a coyote child? Did you spring from the earth? How'd you come to be?"

But I wasn't sure what she meant.

"I live in What Rocks," I told her, "and then L.A., but not now—I'm in What Rocks."

"What rocks? A rock baby, I say. You are a rock baby."

I couldn't tell if she was joking or not.

"My daddy is there," I continued, "and so is Classique and Fashion Jeans and Cut 'N Style and Magic Curl."

"You're gibberish," she said. "You're uncouth, vulgar, I think. I pity you."

We were walking in a clearing of threshed grain, the white straw dry and stalky underfoot.

"Be careful what you do here," she said. "You're on my land. I own this, every inch."

And in that clearing she shook open the quilt, letting the square patterns, all plaid, unfurl and float to the ground. But I couldn't sit on it. She said so. I had to sit in the chaff, which made my shins itchy.

Do you remember the tea parties, Classique? I'd arrange you and the other heads around the folded paper towel, in the tent near the TV. Then I'd pretend-pour tea into your tiny plastic mugs.

"You're my guests," I'd say. "Let me serve you."

The breeze was mussing the quilt, ruffling it over in spots. When I leaned forward to straighten an edge, Dell said, "Don't trouble with it." This was her party. She did the smoothing. She had the linen napkins and Dixie cup. I was the guest of honor.

"Smells good," I said. "I washed my hands too."

She was supposed to tell me how pretty I looked.

"Shush now," she told me. "No more nonsense, that's right."

She removed three foil-covered plates and a thermos from the wicker basket, setting each item at a corner of the quilt. Then she put herself at the center, like a fat jinni riding a magic carpet (the mesh was off her face; she'd already drawn circles in the air, cursed the bees, clapped her hands, spit).

And then she served me, pulling back the foil, choosing carefully with her mittened fingers.

"A bit of this."

A sliver of meat.

"Some of this."

Pound cake.

"Don't spill a drop, you'll get nothing else."

Apple juice.

It wasn't much. But it was good, as I mentioned. A meager feast. Even after finishing my share, I found myself growing fuller while watching Dell. With the napkin on her lap, she ate directly from the plates–all that meat, three slices of pound cake, the thermos was her cup.

But I wasn't bothered, Classique. I was content.

I could hear her breathing, a ragged noise, as her jaws bulged. She wouldn't look at me. And it was like I didn't exist. As if I was the ghost. She just chewed furiously, a mitten gripping the next chunk of food—and it seemed she was speaking to herself, talking with a mouthful, grunting.

The shaded lens of her glasses, coupled with the mumbling, made her a pirate in my mind. The Johnsongrass waving in the distance became an ocean. And we were on a deserted island, and this meal was the treasure. "Argh," I could almost imagine her saying. "Aye! Good booty!"

I belched, expelling the meat's smoky flavor, a pleasant aftertaste. Then I stretched in the chaff and let my eyes close.

Did I fall asleep? I must have. But I awoke to the sound of a quarry boom, noticing that the quilt had vanished. The basket as well. Red ants roamed where the plates had once been, foraging in the grain for leftovers.

And Dell—there she was, her housedress flapping in the wind, the hood blowing to one side; she bustled with her load toward unknown terrain, the dense mesquite cluster at the far-away rim of the clearing. So I followed, keeping several yards behind. I was a spy, secret agent Jeliza-Rose, trailing Pirate Food Woman. Her name wasn't discovered until later.

I'm invisible, I thought. You can't see me. I'm the ghost.

Craggy mesquites sprawled overhead, sheltering a curvy footpath. And I lost sight of Dell, but I heard the happy song she whistled. So I knew she was nearby, further on ahead.

That song. Lift me up to sweet Jesus, and nail me by His crooked cross. My father sometimes sang that song. Oh what a glorious day, to be hung beside my Lord and saved.

And I should've told you this then, Classique. And this is what I want to tell you now—

Dell didn't live in a cave. She wasn't strangled and drowned in a bog, and the queen mother of all fireflies never existed (had I mentioned that?): the light seen in the trees belonged to her home; even during the day the floodlight shone, yellow and bright, above the front door—more as a warning, I suspected, than a welcoming.

Her house was hidden among mesquites, like some decrepit witch's cottage in a fairy tale. But the yard had been tended; there wasn't a single weed. The dirt was tidy too, apparently combed with a rake. And tomatoes and squash grew in beds on either side of a gravel walkway, girdled by odd-shaped rocks.

But, Classique, I saw in the house. And I was careful, tiptoeing along the porch and peeking through an open window—except it wasn't that easy. All the windows were covered. The shades were pulled. It was as if sunlight was the enemy. Still, I managed. One shade was askew, crumpled at the bottom, and—by tilting my head just so—I could see inside.

Maybe, I thought, maybe you're a witch. Or a vampire. Maybe that's why you need the hood, to keep from melting. That's why you forgot me in the clearing, you were beginning to dissolve.

But Dell hadn't dissolved. She was in the dining room, or the living room. I can't remember which. And she no longer wore the hood. And her hands were busy with her hair, bunching it behind her head. Then she took hairpins from her mouth and tucked them into the ball of hair, saying, "Kill a rabbit yourself because I'm too busy today. Do you think you're only person with things to do? I think not. I really don't think you believe that. I really don't."

I couldn't see who she was talking to at first. In fact, other than Dell, I saw little else. The room was dimly lit—impossible to make out—but she stood near the window, fixing her hair beside a table lamp. And I recall thinking that it seemed like nighttime in there, that somehow her clocks must run funny. At night, I imagined, the shades were up and the house glowed from within. Everything was different.

"I can't kill rabbits, Dell, 'cause I can't, you know I can't."

She was Dell. I said it to myself. Dell.

And the person who spoke her name—a man or a boy? I wasn't sure. The voice was sluggish and high, almost girlish.

"You hear me? If I do that to rabbits I feel bad. I don't do that."

A man. He sounded stupid. He sounded like my father, when he pretended to be retarded—when he dragged a leg behind himself on the carpet, chasing me around the apartment. He contorted his lips, asking me, "Jeliza-Rose, are you special too? I a special person, Jeliza-Rose. You love me? You be my friend? I think you're purtty. I your special friend." I hated when he acted like that. I couldn't stand his expression, all twisted and silly. Or how his speech changed, how it became slurred and heavy and sputtering. It was creepy.

"I put food in my tummy already," Dell was saying. "Am I a maid? Am I a wife? Do I make the sky turn blue? Feed yourself, see. You know how, that's right. You're no child, Dickens. I should say not."

And then he appeared, holding a red candle under his narrow chin. Dell kept her back to him; his long face hovered at her shoulder, wearing blue-tinted swimming goggles. She'd called him Dickens, and a wide scar parted his bald scalp, as if he had a hairstyle fashioned from flesh.

"My tummy is empty," he said. "Didn't leave me a crumb. Did you hear that? Didn't even leave me a crumb."

I felt sorry for him. His voice had quivered. He seemed sad, as if he was about to cry.

"Your tummy will get dinner," Dell said. "You'll have rabbit then, see. But not lunch. No lunch. Right, I'll fill you at dinner, okay? But Momma needs reading to before I kill for you."

Then she turned, wandering from the room with him in tow, the candle flickering in the space between them. I remained for a while at the window, listening, but they didn't reappear. And I couldn't hear them anymore. The place was quiet. So I left and headed home.

And that evening at What Rocks, I lied to you, Classique. I told you Dell and Dickens had invited me inside. I said we danced together and played games with cards and sang songs—and Nutter Butters were served from a silver tray. All lies. Dell hadn't fixed the radio, and my father didn't broadcast a message as the three of us held hands (I wouldn't tell you what the message was, because I said it was secret). Dell never whispered that I was her best friend. She never did. She didn't walk me home either. I returned by myself.

But I wasn't lying about the rabbit-hole. You know that, I suppose. At least I think it was a rabbit-hole, found beneath a mesquite tree, several yards from Dell's home. I was on the footpath when I spotted it. And the hole was big enough for my head, but I didn't dare bend over and peer in. Instead I kept a good distance; that way I wouldn't get sucked through.

"She's going to kill you," I told the hole, hoping that if a rabbit was down there it'd hear me. "For dinner she's going to get you, you better hide. They're going to eat you."

Did I tell you that's what I said, Classique? That evening, as we rested by my father's boots, did I mention that I warned the rabbit? Probably not. But I'm letting you know now. And I'm sorry I ever showed you that hole. I really am.

12

My father kept farting, silent but deadly, filling the entire downstairs of What Rocks. The smell was potent, sulfurous—so bad that I had to leave the front door open. But I wasn't worried about the squirrel sneaking in because I knew he'd get a whiff and change his mind. He'd probably pack his squirrel things and head for the hills. And I wouldn't blame him.

"Stop cuttin' muffins! Pooh in the yard because that's where you do it!"

I was in the kitchen, spreading peanut butter on crackers, making lunch for my father, basking in victory: the army ants had finally been defeated; their bodies smushed along the countertop. They'd already dwindled in number—finding less and less to take away—so the decisive battle was easy. And if I hadn't killed them, the farts would have. It was a massacre of mercy.

Cuttin' muffins.

That's what my father called farting.

Or air biscuits.

"In China," he told me, "they got a whole different understanding of things—the louder the burp, the better the meal.

And a powerful air biscuit delivered with grace will get you a free dessert. It's almost an art form there."

"That's gross."

I didn't want to live in China.

And sometimes, when the two of us were eating together, he'd let a fart and then say, "Jeliza-Rose, I can't believe it. You're cuttin' muffins at the dining table. Man, that's nasty."

But it was never me. It was always him. And when I protested, he'd grin and fart again.

"Stop it!"

"Jesus christ," he'd say, pretending to be annoyed, "put a plug in it. I'm trying to eat."

And the madder I got, the more amused he'd become.

"Don't!" I'd scream, verging on tears. "It's you! You're doing it!"

"Whoa, what died in here?"

He'd wave a hand in front of his nose, laughing.

But my mother hated his air biscuits. She'd storm from the kitchen and slam the bedroom door. Or she'd throw something at him, like a spoon or the TV remote control. Once, while she ate at the dining table, he ripped a loud one in the living room—and she hit her fists on the tabletop. She just hit and hit, rattling her fork and frozen dinner and the salt-and-pepper shakers. Then she walked calmly from the room, glaring as she left, not saying a word.

And licking peanut butter off my finger-knife, I was glad my mother wasn't at What Rocks that day. She would've gone crazy for sure, probably yanking his wig and bonnet, slapping him. Then she'd choke him with his ponytail, or bash his skull until it cracked. So it was good she wasn't there, otherwise I'd be preparing lunch for her too; I'd rather smell muffins forever than do that.

"You're a real stinker," I told my father, "and don't say it's me 'cause it's you. And you know it."

His meal waited on the floor—six crackers with peanut butter, three by the left boot, three by the right boot. But he didn't look hungry. In fact, he looked stuffed; the tip of his tongue poked between his scarlet lips, his face was bloated, the rouge had faded some on his puffed cheeks.

"What're you eating? You're all big. That's why you're farting too. And you're fat—your belly is poking."

I imagined him rising from the chair in the middle of the night—his boots creaking on the floorboards—and going outside to a cache of candy bars and Little Debbie Snack Cakes, his favorites.

"Daddy, you can have crackers tonight," I said, spotting my reflection in his sunglasses. "You don't have to have them now if you don't want to. But I made them for you so—"

I cupped a hand across my mouth, horrified:

The Bog Man was on the front porch; his footsteps thudded against the slats, briskly. Peeping around the chair, I glimpsed his tall figure darting by the open doorway, heard his footsteps thumping further along the porch, where they stopped abruptly outside the living room window. And then he was gazing in at me—I almost saw him from the corner of my eyes—but I couldn't look.

Clutching my father's clammy hand I yelled, "You go away! Go! You go! Leave me alone!"

His high-pitched voice was muffled behind the panes.

"Oh no, I'm sorry, no!"

Dickens. That was his name. It was him.

"She's isn't here anymore, I know that," he said, alarmed. "I'm going. Don't be mad, please. I'm wrong again. She's isn't here anymore."

I glanced sideways, catching sight of him, shirtless and boney. And he was frightened, I could tell.

He was hugging himself.

"What do you want?"

With the blue goggles pushed up on his forehead, he was nodding at me and my father while stepping from the window. Then he turned and ran, flashing past the doorway, saying, "I'm sorry, I'm sorry! I thought she was here!" His footsteps pounded the slats, banged the steps, and then crunched quickly through the yard.

And without thinking I tore after him.

Jumping the bottom porch step into the yard, I shouted, "Dickens, don't be scared! Dell is my friend! We ate a picnic too!"

He was already hurrying toward the cattle trail, glancing back every so often with a spooked expression. He moved like those athletes on TV, those Olympic walkers, the ones my father and I always laughed at–foot in front of foot, elbows swinging out, head straight. And he couldn't run very fast because of the flip-flop sandals clomping under his feet.

"Dickens!"

Flip-flops and green swimming trunks, skin as white as a saltine, he wasn't scary at all.

"I'm Dell's best friend!"

When I reached the grazing pasture, he was nowhere to be seen. He'd been right in front of me on the winding trail, but now he was gone. And so I stood where the trail ended, searching the pasture ahead, the bus, the weeds beyond.

Scotty beamed you up, I thought.

Then I caught his breathing, all congested and difficult, like his nostrils were filled with snot. He was nearby, crouching in the Johnsongrass. The goggles showed among the sorghum. And I could see his eyes, wide and alert, fixed on me.

"Come out," I said, parting the grass. "I see you."

Dickens shook. His knees were at his chin, and he stared down at his flip-flops with embarrassment. He smacked his lips but said nothing.

"I know who you are."

His head tilted slightly up.

"If I run too fast," he said quietly, out of breath, "I faint like a girl."

He had a small boy's voice and face, an old man's body.

"I'm a girl," I told him, "and I don't faint like a girl."

"Oh," he said, "I guess you're different."

"I think so," I said. "I'm Jeliza-Rose. My daddy wrote a song about me because I'm special."

The sorghum enclosed us as I squatted before him, bringing my knees under my chin. I was on safari in the jungle. And Dickens was an African scout, an albino. Deeper in the Johnsongrass lurked tigers and lions.

He closed an eye, touched the goggles on his forehead. "How come you know my name?"

"That's 'cause Dell told me. She's my best friend."

"She's my sister," he said. "You're the vandal. You're the What Rocks baby, she said that."

"Tell me about it. And I thought she was the ghost, and I thought you were the Bog Man. I thought you were him until I saw you."

"No, I'm not that man. I don't even know what that man is."

"He lives in the ground. He's waiting in Jutland."

"Oh. Was that your mom?"

"My daddy," I said. "He's sleeping, I guess. That's all he does."

"Oh. He's pretty too."

"I know. Me and Classique made him pretty."

Dickens' head wobbled. His eyes were half-closed as he inhaled.

Then he glanced at me, making a careless pattern in the dirt with his fingers, saying, "The old lady lived there, at What Rocks. That was when I was little. See, the door was open. She could've been there too, but I knew she wasn't but maybe she was. I'm always getting in trouble that way, when I'm wrong."

His toenails were yellow. The scar on his bald head was pink like a blister.

"What happened to your head?"

"Nothing—except when I was little they cut inside. Well, I wasn't that little. But when I was younger they did because I'm epileptic. Couldn't even mow a lawn. So they cut my brain. Now I have two brains so I'm not epileptic no more, only sometimes."

"What is it?"

"Like this—"

He rolled his eyes into his skull. His body began twitching. His hands rose, trembling. Then he stopped and rubbed at the scar.

"See, only sometimes it happens since this."

I didn't know what to say, so I asked, "Do you have a pool?"

"No. Can't swim. I'll drown. Can't splash in pools or drive a car. Can't bowl either."

"I don't swim. In the tub I do. But I don't drive cars or bowl."

"Me either. I get a seizure then I sink in the pool like a penny. I get a seizure and the bowling ball smashes my feet. I drived before but that was bad and if I do it now Dell says I get arrested or worse. So I can't drive to save my life, not even if I'm bloody or my arm's chopped off."

"If you drive you'll go–"

I rolled my eyes and twitched for a moment.

"Yeah. That's what'll happen all right."

Then we both smiled. And in the silence that followed we fidgeted, inarticulate, and dug patterns in the dirt.

The Johnsongrass swayed overhead and around, murmuring.

"Say, I was meaning to say," Dickens finally said, "I've got a submarine. It's big enough for me. See, then I don't have to swim anyway."

"Can I play in it?"

At first he said sure, and then he went, "I don't know, maybe tomorrow you can. I don't know."

"But I'd like to see it because I like submarines. And maybe you'd play in it with me."

"I guess. Thing is, you've got to hold my hand, okay? Then you can come with me there."

"Okay."

"That way we don't get lost from each other."

"Okay."

He extended a slender hand. So I took it. And his palm was warmer than mine. Then he led the way, trudging through the Johnsongrass, trampling stalks, where hoppers sprang from underfoot like tiny land mines. And as we wandered parallel with the grazing pasture–the hull of the school bus looming–I said, "Fireflies visit me in the bus at nighttime."

Dickens squeezed my hand.

"That's a bad place," he said, sounding fearful. "It's wrong there."

But I didn't ask why.

You're a sissy, I thought. That's how come you talk like that. That's how come you're scared all the time.

A hopper clung to my shin; I let it ride on me until we left the sorghum–then I slapped it dead.

Dickens was saying, "I've got a million pennies."

We were side-by-side, stepping between railroad ties. And I kept looking back in case a train was coming.

"I'll show you."

He released my hand and began walking faster, leaving me behind, his flip-flops going clomp clomp clomp. His butt jiggled in the trunks. It was funny. His legs were hairy and skinny. He reminded me of a flamingo, a white flamingo.

"You're a bird!"

"Not really," he said, bending on the tracks, pointing at a rail. "A bird doesn't have pennies, but I've got lots."

And he did have lots. They were on the rail, pressed into flat blobs of copper; hundreds of them–fused, overlapping–stretching for yards.

"You're rich."

"I will be. Because someday they'll get squished together and make a big penny. The world's biggest penny. Do you know how much that'll be?"

"A million dollars."

"At least. And I'll buy a boat then. Or a real submarine–"

A real submarine? He reached for my hand.

"–that's much better than the one I got."

But he didn't have a submarine to show me. It was a wigwam built from mesquite branches and weeds, in the embankment beside the tracks. And it was packed with junk–a mangled bicycle, smashed cans, three shredded tires. There wasn't room to play or sit. There wasn't even a periscope.

"She's Lisa," he told me, pulling the goggles to his eyes. "Vessels underwater have girl names. Boats on top do too. Well, some of them do."

I asked about the bicycle, with its twisted frame and crushed spokes.

"Shark attack."

And the tires. And the cans.

"Monster shark."

Then he explained.

The junk was bait. He was a great shark hunter, exploring the South Pacific in his submarine. Mostly he used pennies for bait, but sometimes he found bigger lure for his prey. Then he hid in the wigwam and waited. And soon the monster shark came gliding along the tracks, jaws thrashing, mashing anything in its path–a bicycle, beer cans, old tires, helpless pennies. Nothing escaped.

"The only way to kill that shark is to blow it up," he said. "Rocks and spears don't work, believe me. I'm lucky I'm alive."

His voice suddenly sounded deep, not sissy. He cocked an eyebrow. And I thought he seemed brave, and older–like a captain. But when the cowbell clanked in the distance, he became Dickens again.

"Uh-oh," he said. "I need to be home. You too. You can't be in here without me. It's my submarine."

He grabbed my hand and we ducked out of the wigwam.

The cowbell continued clanking and clanking.

And Dell was somewhere shouting: "Dickens! Home! Dickens! Home! Dickens–"

"We can play tomorrow," he said, letting go of my hand. "Don't get in my submarine without me!"

Then he scurried away–foot in front of foot, elbows swinging, head straight, clomp clomp.

"Bye, friend!" I called after him, waving. "Don't drown!"

But he didn't turn and wave. He didn't say anything as he went.

"Come visit me tomorrow!"

And I knew Dell had pound cake for him. And apple juice. She probably had the picnic basket all ready. My stomach grumbled.

After that I returned to What Rocks—"Stinky Fart Rocks," I said to myself—where my father's lunch had been stolen, carted past the open door by a robber. Cracker crumbs were scattered across the living room floor, morsels for the ants to claim. And the squirrel rampaged on the roof, chattering and creating a racket—his teeth, I imagined, smeared with peanut butter.

13

Dickens didn't come for me the next day.

I ate saltines on the porch steps and waited, listening to the noisy cicadas, hoping that a quarry boom would suddenly erupt and silence them for a while. Then I played Shark Attack with Classique. She was a goldfish on my fingertip, swimming in front of me while I chomped at her.

"Don't eat me! Don't eat me!"

"Grrrrrrrrrrrrrr–!"

And when I put her in my mouth she tasted worse than cough syrup. Some strands of her hair got under my tongue, and I had to spit them out. Then I kept spitting until I couldn't taste her anymore.

"You're gross," I told her. "You're dirty."

"You love Dickens," she said.

"No, I don't! How do you know?"

"You love him because he's a shark hunter. You want to kiss the cut on his head and hold hands."

"And he has a submarine too."

"Except it's fake."

"But he's going to be rich and buy a real one. He has

more pennies than you. But I won't show you if you don't shut up that I love him, Classique, because I don't really."

Dickens was a flamingo. He walked funny. But he hunted the monster shark. And he was my friend.

"He's a sissy."

"Sometimes he's a captain too."

In Lisa he roamed the South Pacific. Perhaps he appeared on TV—that's where I always saw boats and oceans and submarines and sharks. I might've seen him on PBS—his submersible exploring the remains of the Titanic—and didn't even know it was Dickens at the helm.

"He's sailing under the seas."

"So he's not coming."

"But maybe he will."

"Maybe he forgot where What Rocks is—"

"And he's searching."

"Because we're in danger."

What Rocks was sinking fast; it'd just hit an iceberg. Soon I'd be swallowing saltwater. So would Classique. We had to stay afloat until Dickens rescued us. He was our only hope.

"Come on," I said. "Don't give up. We have to swim for dry land."

"But I can't swim."

"Dog paddle," I said. "Dog paddle like the wind!"

We drifted from the steps—my arms parting the waves—and let the tide carry us away. Then we were underwater, gliding past the seaweed-sorghum. I held my breath for as long as possible. But it was hard. So I transformed into an octopus, my fingers fluttering like tentacles. Classique became a seahorse. And in the grazing pasture, we swam around the upturned Titanic, where minnow-hoppers darted in and out of the busted windows.

"It sank to the bottom of the sea," I told Classique, gazing into the murky interior of the wreck.

"No one survived," she said. "It's spooky."

"Let's go."

We floated over the rise to see if Dell was in her meadow.

But she wasn't. So we swam off–eventually surfacing by the tracks, panting for air near Dickens' wigwam. We'd almost drowned.

"The monster shark could be anywhere," I told Classique, stooping. "We better be on the lookout."

The squashed pennies stretched along the rail like misshapen drops from a candle. And I tried peeling one up, but it wouldn't budge. The shark had crushed it good and proper.

"It's dangerous here. We're safer in the submarine."

I imagined the shark racing forward, teeth snapping as it sailed after us.

"Shark attack!" I yelled.

And Classique and I scrambled across the tracks, down the embankment, and into Lisa. But Dickens wasn't waiting inside. He wasn't at the helm, goggles in place, searching the ocean floor for What Rocks and me. And the wigwam didn't seem any more like a submarine than it had the day before.

"Shark attack"

Lisa was falling to pieces, and Classique hated her. She thought the wigwam smelled worse than What Rocks. With all the junk and the dirt, she thought Lisa was more of a wreck than the bus; part of the shotgun roof had caved in overnight, several long mesquite branches lay crosswise on the crunched bicycle, other branches covered the shredded tires, others stood vertical–stabbing the ground and jutting out the gap in the roof. The collapse sliced the wigwam in half, making the already confined interior more cramped.

Lisa's been sunk, I thought. Dickens can't swim. He isn't even an octopus or a seahorse.

"The pirate did it," Classique said. "She boarded the submarine and took him prisoner. The captain will walk the plank for sure. She'll drown him because she's a pig. She left you in the field. She's trouble."

And Dell came to mind–pound cake in one hand, her lips wet with apple juice, her dark lens glinting in the afternoon sunlight. She was out there somewhere, waving a sword above her head–"Aye! Aye!"–or pressing the tip of the sword against Dickens' spine as his flip-flops clomped toward the end of a plank.

"Save him! Save the captain–"

"–or he's shark food!"

But we didn't have to save Dickens after all. He was fine, mumbling to himself and smiling, raking the front yard of his and Dell's home. And he wasn't in flip-flops or a swimming suit. The goggles weren't on his forehead. He had on a red baseball cap and a T-shirt. He wore jeans and cowboy boots. He looked like a farmer.

"He's not a captain or a prisoner–"

"–or anything."

Classique and I were cloistered among mesquites, spying behind a juniper bush, watching as Dickens went in circles. He kept going around and around, raking his bootprints, mumbling and smiling, mumbling and smiling. He couldn't get it right. Soon as a patch was raked, he'd turn and step backwards into it. His bootprints were everywhere.

And Dell was there too, wearing her hood and mittens, picking tomatoes and squash in her garden, setting the vegetables into a plastic bag, tossing some aside. And she was whistling to herself. But every now and then she'd pause, telling Dickens, "No, no, see–you've forgotten a spot, of course. Pay attention."

She'd point, jabbing a finger.

"Not there–there."

And Dickens would scan the dirt, searching for what he'd missed. He'd step backwards, creating new bootprints.

"Right there. Yes, right there."

Then he'd rake nervously at the bootprints before him, mumbling and smiling, mumbling and smiling.

"No, no, see–now there's more. You're messing it all up as you go. Pay attention, right?"

It could've continued for hours–Dell pointing, Dickens raking and making fresh bootprints–except Patrick the Bagger Boy arrived in his Nissan. The horn honked twice as the pickup truck came bouncing over the bumpy driveway, sunlight reflecting off the windshield.

The honks startled Dickens; he let the rake fall. Then, biting his bottom lip, he glanced at Dell and hugged himself.

"Uh-oh," he said.

She stood upright on the gravel walkway and told him, "Go in. Stay in your room until I call you out."

"Okay, Dell, okay."

Off he went, running like crazy, still hugging himself. His boots pounded the ground, leaving more prints in the dirt. He jumped onto the porch, and, once inside the house, he slammed the front door.

"They'll stay far."

Dell drew a ring in the air. Then she clapped her hands. Then she removed the hood and helmet, placing them on the walkway, and spit into the yard.

"They'll mess elsewhere."

The Nissan had already pulled in alongside the house–the driver's door standing wide open. And Patrick, straining, was busy lifting two heavy paper sacks from the bed. Then he cradled them, one in each arm, and walked around to the yard, where Dell was wiping her mittens across her apron.

"After-noon, M-m-m-iss Munro," Patrick said.

"Hello, Patrick," Dell said. "Is it afternoon? My how the day flies, you know."

She was grinning. Her voice had a friendly tone. She seemed like someone else, someone younger.

"Yes, m-m-m-am, sure does!"

Dell aimed a finger at the porch.

"You can put your load there, by the door. I can bring the sacks in myself. You remembered Land O Lakes–sweet and unsalted, yes? And the buffalo jerky?"

He nodded. He was grinning too.

"Of course, you remembered, yes, yes."

She watched as he set the sacks on the porch, lightly touching her hair, the yellow bun.

"I appreciate all you do for me, Patrick. You're such a kind young man."

Then he was going to her on the walkway, smirking from one side of his mouth. She reached for his hand, took it, and held it against her chest.

He stammered, "I-I-I-I–"

"I know," she said, "you already paid for everything."

He nodded.

"Right, yes, of course. Thank you, thank you."

"W-w-w-will you?" he asked.

"Yes, Patrick, I will. But not here, not in the yard, not by the tomatoes."

What happened next I didn't understand. Neither did Classique. It didn't make any sense.

Dell led Patrick to the side of the house, where she had him stretch out on the ground. Then she knelt down beside him. He rested a hand on her yellow bun as she unzipped his pants. And his eyes shut, his lips parted. She found his boy-thingy and held it–ugly thingy, swollen and purple. And she kissed it, put it in her mouth for a bit. He was moving her head with his hand–back and forth, back and forth–gripping her bun. It was like Dell was eating something big, her cheeks were puffed. She was hungry.

Back and forth.

Patrick was breathing hard, moaning a little bit.

She's hurting him, I thought. She's sucking his blood.

Then Dell suddenly quit. She stood and straddled him, lifting her dress, bunching the hem in her mittens. And she squatted, pretending she was a rider and Patrick was a horse. She moved her hips around, but didn't say anything. She wasn't laughing or smiling, just riding along quietly. But Patrick's fingers were scratching at the dirt. His sneakers twisted, and his lips trembled like he wanted to yell, like he just couldn't get the words out–"H-h-h-h-h-help!" But he never screamed, only groaned and thrust upward some. His face was flushed as he uttered, "Oh, sh-sh-shit, oh–!"

And that was it. Dell was done playing. She climbed from him, letting her hem fall around her boots. But Patrick remained on the ground, exhausted, his thingy still sticking from his pants.

She's a vampire, Classique thought. You're next.

And I didn't want Dell doing that to me, draining my blood, putting her mouth between my legs, or riding me.

"It's gross," I whispered.

So we began sneaking away, but a juniper twig snagged my dress. When I yanked free, the bush rustled. Then we ran. We flew past the mesquites. And I worried that Dell had heard me, that she and Patrick might be chasing after me.

Eventually, I stopped behind a tree and looked. But no one was coming. Her house was in the distance. Just then Patrick's Nissan honked twice. He was leaving. And I figured they hadn't spotted me running away.

I took a deep breath.

That rabbit-hole is nearby, Classique was thinking. Why don't you show me it. You're safe from them, I think.

If I do, you'll have to listen for her. She could trap us.

No, she won't. She didn't hear you. You escaped.

"Okay," I said. "All right."

Then I wandered to the footpath, glancing around every so often for Dell. The rabbit-hole was easy to find, a cavernous opening beneath the mesquite tree. And I showed it to Classique, my arm extended. I held her over the brink. The hole was black, much larger than I remembered. I could maybe squeeze my shoulders past the rim.

Closer, Jeliza-Rose. Let me go in.

But the rabbit is there.

Closer, please.

"This is Alice's hole," I said.

And just then Classique slipped. In she went. Spinning, spinning, spinning into blackness, beyond my reach. Lost. She was falling through the earth, to where the people walked with their heads downwards.

My stomach sank like Lisa.

"Classique!"

And I wanted to cry. And I would've too—but she sent a

message: "It's okay, dear. I'm falling very slowly. The sides of the hole are filled with cupboards and book-shelves. I wonder how many miles I've fallen by this time?"

I couldn't go home. Not yet. So I stayed there until dusk, in the golden light, wondering how to rescue her. I sat under the mesquite tree with my legs crossed. I tossed pebbles into the creepy hole. Then the train whistle blew. And I knew the Bog Man would soon be stirring in his grave.

"Classique, don't worry," I said.

But no message came.

She's sleeping, I told myself. She's sleeping, flying down down down, dreaming of me and What Rocks and her bodiless friends.

And wandering home that evening, I was angry at myself for finding the rabbit-hole in the first place. And mad at Classique too. She wanted me to take her closer. It was her fault anyway—now I was alone again.

"You're so stupid," I said. "Sometimes you're the dumbest."

14

Classique was the first head I discovered in the thrift shop
bin. I held her in my palm and showed my mother.

"She's so beautiful," I said.

My mother shrugged. She wasn't looking at me. She was
gazing at a shelf lined with painted china plates, all mounted
on wire stands, each depicting a different image—a waterfall,
John Wayne, kittens, Jesus on the cross, The Beatles.

"Can I have her, please?"

And to my surprise, my mother said yes. She dug two dollars from her purse.

"If it's more than that," she said, "put it back."

She hadn't read the cardboard sign above the bin: All
Doll Parts, Mix & Match, 5 for $1.

"Thank you, thank you," I said.

Then—carefully holding Classique in a hand—I rummaged
through the box of arms and torsos and legs and heads. I
found Magic Curl next. Then Fashion Jeans. Then Cut 'N
Style. But none of them were as good or as beautiful as
Classique. She was the best. And she knew it.

"Dear, I picked you," she told me later. "And you picked

the others."

If her voice had a flavor it would've been honey, sweet and ingratiating.

But after falling into the hole, it became harder to hear her. Her voice was fainter, a distant transmission almost impossible to make out, and sometimes she had to scream. "CAN YOU HEAR ME NOW?! CAN YOU–?!"

While I slept on my father's mattress, she appeared; her red hair billowed as she sailed past cupboards and bookcases, her tight lips somewhere between a grimace and a smile.

"This is it, dear. I'm done for. You've abandoned me, I suppose."

No, you'll be okay. I need you.

"Too late. Too late. But at least you have the others for company."

The others; they were on the floor when I awoke the next morning, waiting anxiously like beauty queens at the conclusion of a pageant. Three heads wondering which among them would replace Classique and receive the crown of Jeliza-Rose's friendship.

"She's not dead yet," I told them. "You're just sharks! You're happy she's falling through the earth!"

Then I forbade them to speak for a million years.

"You're just heads! You don't have hearts! You're traitors!"

I attacked on hands and knees, tucking my index finger behind my thumb–and then I flicked the traitors around the room.

"Take that–!"

Flick.

Magic Curl spun across the floor like a top.

"And you–!"

Flick.

Fashion Jeans shot up into the air.

"And you too–!"

But I couldn't flick Cut 'N Style.

My finger hesitated in front of her damaged face and blackened eyeballs. If anyone had a right to hate Classique it was Cut 'N Style—so I tipped her over, gently, and whispered in her ear, "You're better than those other two. I'm sorry Classique was so mean to you."

Then I considered bringing her with me to the rabbit-hole, where I could put her on Grandmother's boa and lower her inside. And because Cut 'N Style was blind, maybe she'd be good at sensing Classique there in the darkness. Maybe she could somehow rescue Classique and they'd be best friends for life.

I want to save her, Cut 'N Style was thinking. Let me come.

"No, you better stay," I concluded, reluctantly. "You might fall in—then I'd be trapped with Fashion Jeans and Magic Curl. They're just as bad as ants. They're worse than squirrels."

And I was glad Cut 'N Style didn't accompany me after all. She wouldn't have been much help. The boa was point-less as well, too light and fluffy for a lifeline; I couldn't tell if it was reaching anything in the hole or not.

"Dumb big feathers!"

I ended up slinging the boa around my neck—while Classique screamed from the void—and went searching for something else, something long and sturdy.

CAN YOU HEAR ME?!

Yes. Loud and clear.

IT'S COLD! I'VE HIT BOTTOM, I'M PRETTY SURE! OR I'M ON A LEDGE PERHAPS!

Don't worry. I'm here. I'm getting a stick.

IT'S SO VERY COLD AND I'M SO TIRED—!

"I'm coming," I said. "Don't go to sleep. Stay awake."

Mesquite branches were everywhere, on the ground, beside the footpath, all gangly and brittle; none was long enough though. I had to break a dead branch from a tree, had to tug on one end of it until the slender limb splintered loose in my fist. Then I dragged it on the footpath.

Branch longer than my leg, I thought. Longer than P-P-Patrick's creepy boy-thingy.

And I felt like whistling as the branch scratched against

the dirt. I pursed my lips, blowing. But only breath and some saliva burbled from me. It was hopeless.

So I invented a happy song instead.

I sang, "Dragging the branch, dragging the branch–better watch out for Mr. Dragon Branch–he'll bite your head, he'll bite your head–dragging the branch–Mr. Dragon Branch–dragging the branch–"

It was such a great song that I leaned over the hole, smiling, and began singing for Classique, the words echoing in the blackness. I pretended that all the nearby mesquites were an audience of old men and old women. They were applauding; their craggy twig-fingers wore diamond rings and gold bands.

I finished with, "Thank you, everyone, everyone everywhere," and stroked the boa like it was a cat sitting on my shoulders.

And when the applause finally died in my mind, I listened for Classique's faint message. She was supposed to say, "Fantastic! You're wonderful! Mr. Dragon Branch is the bestest song ever!"

But she didn't say anything.

"Classique," I said, "are you still there?"

No message arrived.

I waited.

"Classique–?"

Nothing.

I stuck the branch into the hole. Down down down. Three feet, at least. My hand and wrist slid past the rim. And suddenly the branch stabbed the bottom–crunching against soil, perhaps poking clods and pebbles–and broke apart. Then it was as if the earth caved in, the hole became deeper.

"Uh-oh," I said, sounding like Dickens.

I couldn't poke the bottom anymore, just space. So I opened my hand, letting what remained of the branch drop.

"He's coming!" I warned Classique.

Mr. Dragon Branch was falling toward her now. He'll bite her head, he'll bite her head.

Then I sat with my legs crossed and contemplated the hole. Classique hadn't tumbled as far as I thought. If I had grown-up arms, I could reach in there and probably touch her with my fingertips. And I wouldn't be afraid of the darkness inside—the hole wouldn't look so huge.

"Uh-oh," I said again.

I imagined Dickens hugging himself with those skinny arms, his hands almost meeting at his spine. He could rescue her in a heartbeat. His arms were like broom handles. He didn't need a rake, he could comb the yard with his fingers. He wouldn't even have to bend much.

"Classique, I'll be back."

I had an idea.

"Don't go anywhere."

Dickens didn't need the rake. But I did. And the rake wouldn't crumble; its claws could go into the hole—snagging Classique and bits of the branch and clods and pebbles—and come out again in one piece.

The Rake of Life, I thought—wandering along the footpath, sneakers stepping over stones. Making my way to the edge of Dell's front yard, I glanced around cautiously. Dell might be hiding nearby, lurking behind a grizzled trunk; she'd suck my blood if I wasn't careful.

"You'll stay far," I said.

I turned and spit.

"You'll mess elsewhere."

Crouching at the juniper bush, I scanned the yard, the walkway, the porch. The yellow light glowed above the front door. But the Rake of Life was gone. And everything was silent. No whistling, no mumbling. The house seemed deserted—shades pulled, dim—like Dell and Dickens had packed their bags and went on vacation. Or they were napping. Or exploring the ocean in Lisa.

I left the bush and crossed the yard, leaving prints where Dickens had raked. And I crept alongside the house, going to the backyard—my ears listening for anything, a whisper, a voice, floorboards creaking.

It was another world, the backyard; it wasn't tidy like the front. Weeds and foxtails grew high. A blue Ford pickup was parked near the house, a crack zigzagging across the windshield. Further off stood a storage shed without windows—all corrugated iron, even the walls and door—and beside it, netted with chicken wire, were two wooden hutches.

But where was the Rake of Life? There was nothing else on my mind.

As I headed for the shed, a blast erupted somewhere in the mesquites—in the distance—breaking the silence, startling me for a second. A second blast. A third. Not the same booms as from the quarry. Different, less thunderous. These blasts weren't as scary.

I followed a beaten trail—the weeds no doubt matted by Dell's boots—and peered into the brambles, squinting, looking for the rake. But the overgrowth was too dense. I couldn't see the ground.

Where'd they put you? Maybe in here, maybe—

I rattled the padlock on the shed door, but it was fastened. A strong odor lingered about the place, distinctive, turpentine or nail polish remover. My eyes burned some. And I couldn't tell if the rake was inside. I tried peeking through a thin gap between the door and its frame. Impossible. The shed was as dark as the hole.

The search had been a complete failure, so I uttered my father's favorite curse: "Shit fuck fire!"

I kicked the shed door.

Things and people kept disappearing. Classique. The bottom of the hole. Dell and Dickens. The rake. Even the hutches were bare, except for stained newspaper and chunks of white fur and pellet-sized turds.

"Shit fuck fire!"

There was no escaping it; I had to return to the hole empty-handed. And that's what I did, with pouting lips, swinging my arms limply, punting stones from the footpath—the vision of defeat.

What's worse, I couldn't remember my song. I slumped in front of the hole and tried singing it.

"Dragon Branch coming–Mr. Dragon Branch–he'll bite her head–"

But the words weren't correct, neither was the rhythm.

"–Mr. Dragon Branch coming–coming coming–"

It was useless, so I quit trying and slapped my forehead. And that's when I heard the boy say, "–hell, I don't know, Luke. You were there first."

And another boy said, "I know, I know."

They were half-laughing, talking loud, getting closer. Then I saw them. They strolled right by me and the mesquite tree and the hole, going leisurely on the footpath toward Dell's house. But they didn't notice me. They were too busy chatting and staring forward. One had black jeans, one had blue jeans. Both carried bolt-action rifles. And they seemed like wild boys, twins or brothers–baseball caps pulled low, tanned necks, pants tucked into muddy boots–tank tops hanging loosely, showing whiter than white skin beneath the neckline.

Black Jeans' rifle barrel was propped on a shoulder. Two dead rabbits hung from his belt; their hind paws bound with wire. And Blue Jeans was chewing something, gum maybe, or tobacco; he held his rifle at his hip, the barrel pointing downward.

"Hey, you sure we ain't lost, Luke?" Blue Jeans was saying.

"Positive. This'll take us to the road. I'm positive."

I went to the footpath and watched them go. The backsides of their britches were green with grass stains. Black Jeans tugged at his rear as if his butt itched, as if his underwear had bunched in his crack. Then I pursued them for a while–a glamorous spy with a boa, keeping a safe distance, eventually concealing myself among trees. They were nearing Dell's house, chattering like squirrels, making a racket.

Better be quiet, I thought. You'll get your blood sucked.

And no sooner had it crossed my mind when Dell appeared.

"Vandals," she screamed. "Yes, yes, stay put!"

She sprang from the woods, scrambling onto the footpath—her housedress flapping, the hood and helmet askew. And both boys started. And if Dell wasn't holding a smoothbore shotgun—aiming the lengthy barrel, swinging it back and forth, from one boy to the other—they might've bolted. But they didn't. They didn't move an inch.

"Criminals and filth," she shrieked. "Do you know where you are, trespassers?"

"No, no, we was going to the road, to Keeler's place," Black Jeans began suddenly. "We was takin' a shortcut."

"Liar!" Dell yelled. "What kin are you of Willy Keeler? None, I think!"

She thrust the barrel like it was a pitchfork, piercing the air between herself and the boys.

"He's my uncle," Blue Jeans began, "I swear it," and his voice wavered.

"Mine too," Black Jeans said.

"Mine too, mine too!" Dell mocked. "I swear it, I swear it!"

"We're visiting, honestly," Blue Jeans explained. "We didn't know we was trespassing."

"There wasn't no sign or a fence or anything," said Black Jeans.

Dell continued jabbing the shotgun at them.

"Of course, right, and this shortcut is your shortcut? This is where you go? I think not. I own this land. It's mine. All of it. And those are mine!"

She was pushing the mouth of the sleek barrel at Black Jeans, shoving it at the rabbits hanging on his belt.

"Those there, mine! Understand? They belong to me!"

Black Jeans' voice seemed about to crack. "We're sorry," he murmured. "We didn't know."

Dell sneered.

"Yes, I should say so," she said. "The pair of you are sorry. I've seen everything, right? I've been watching you, filthy, filthy. Peeing on my land, blowing your noses on your shirts. Hunting here!"

And afterwards—when everything was finished—I spoke

into the hole, hoping Classique could hear me, telling her that the boys were lucky Dell didn't murder them.

"You cross my path again," she'd said, "you'll regret it for certain. I'm worse than death."

That's what I told Classique: "They got lucky–Dell's meaner than death."

I lay on my stomach beside the hole–hands folded under my chin, the boa sandwiched in my palms–and related the entire episode. I mentioned that Dell had the boys unload their rifles, that she took their bullets and their rabbits. And the boys were shaking and nervous the whole time. But Dell didn't suck them. She just warned them with her froggy voice.

"You cross my path again–"

Then she let them go; they rushed from the footpath, bounding through the woods like deer, boots crackling on twigs, vanishing.

"And I'm probably invisible," I said. "Dell didn't see me, Classique, 'cause I'm almost a ghost. I really think I am, don't you?"

I stared into the hole, waiting for an answer that never came.

So I closed my eyes and sent psychic messages: You there? Can you hear me? Am I loud and clear?

Nothing except static, a far-off hiss.

I needed the radio. I could use the dial to find Classique, to tune her in. Then maybe I could remember my song. And she'd enjoy hearing me sing, a special broadcast just for her. She'd stay awake and listen. And she wouldn't feel so lonely– my song would keep her warm in the hole.

15

Dickens came for me with a pocketful of bullets, and I thought he was the squirrel at first. I was upstairs and heard him stomping around below. And because I'd opened the front door that afternoon–letting in fresh air, clearing out some of my father's stink–I was sure it was the squirrel in the living room, rummaging about, searching for crackers and peanut butter.

But when going downstairs to investigate, I found Dickens–shirtless, in jeans and flip-flops–standing in front of my father, gazing with the blue goggles on.

"Hi," I said, stepping up behind the leather chair.

He glanced at me, flinching. And I expected him to start hugging himself. But he didn't.

"I'm sorry," he began. "I better go–I didn't knock and that's rude–and it's getting late already–so I'll go, okay?"

His fists tightened. He seemed like the squirrel, jittery and ready to dash for the door.

"You don't have to go," I told him.

"Oh," he said, nodding, "that's good–'cause I was thinking you should play with me today, okay?"

"Okay," I said.

And just then I wanted to ask if he'd rescue Classique. I was about to say that his skinny arms could stretch deep inside any hole in the world. But before I had the chance, he said, "Your daddy sleeps a lot. My momma does too. That's all she ever does these days."

I tried imagining Dickens' mom, but Dell filled my mind instead; she was sleeping somewhere in that dim house, or sitting still in a chair, the hood and helmet resting on her lap.

Where was his mother?

"Is she a ghost?"

He shook his head.

"Not anymore, not really–she's just a dozer. She's isn't as pretty as your daddy. Her hair isn't nice like his is."

"It's only fake," I said. "Look–"

I reached over the chair and tugged on the bonnet and blond wig, lifting them a bit.

"That's funny," he said, flatly. "You fooled me 'cause I didn't know."

"Not supposed to be funny," I replied, straightening the wig, smoothing the coils. "It was Classique's idea anyway, it wasn't my idea. And now she's in the hole and I can't get her."

Dickens pinched his nostrils, fanned the air with a hand.

"He's spoiled," he said, his voice sounding nasally. "He must've been sleeping forever."

"He's cuttin' muffins is all."

"Oh. I guess that's what it is, I guess. Whatever it is–"

Then he dug in a pocket, removing six bullets. He held them in his palm for me to see.

"I can feed the shark these," he said. "If you want, you can help me too. We can't catch the shark with these but we can lure it."

He let me hold one;–gold-colored, rounded at the tip, longer than my fingers. I rubbed the bottom of the shell, remembering how Dell made the hunters unload their rifles. I figured she'd given the bullets to Dickens–or maybe he stole them when she wasn't looking.

"All right," I said, "I'll help you, but you have to help me later. You have to rescue my friend."

"I don't know," he said. "I probably can't do it."

"It won't be hard, I promise. She's in trouble. She'll get hurt bad if you can't save her."

"Maybe she's hurt already."

"Or she's dying. She's farther than the ocean, I think."

"Uh-oh," he said. "That's farther than the moon."

"And you're better than a stick or a rake—you're the captain!"

"Yeah, I am. I've got my own submarine."

"I know."

"Her name is Lisa."

"I know. Will you help me?"

"Can we feed the shark? I'd like to do that. I'd like to play with you too."

"Then you'll rescue my friend."

Dickens shrugged.

"If you'll show me what to do," he said, "in case I don't understand everything about it."

"Yes."

He popped his knuckles and sucked his lip and tilted his head and sighed.

"Okay," he finally said, moving toward me. "Okay," putting his slender hand in my hand.

And off we went—through the front door, along the porch—escaping the flatulence of What Rocks. Across the yard. Into the sorghum. Swishing among the grass. Climbing to the tracks. Moving into the tideland, going underwater. Dickens couldn't have known this—I was an octopus, he was swimming like a dolphin. If I told him, he might've panicked. Then he'd drown for certain and Classique would never be saved. So I didn't mention that we were beneath the sea, or that there were men miles above us fishing.

Dickens said, "You get three."

Three bullets, clanking in my palm.

We crouched on the tracks, downwind from Lisa and the flattened pennies.

"Put them here this way—"

He carefully set each of his bullets on the rail, crosswise, spacing them apart by a foot or so. Then he watched as I did the same on the opposite rail.

"What'll happen?" I asked.

Dickens puffed his cheeks. He made an erupting noise and clapped his hands together.

"The end of the world," he said.

"The monster shark will die?"

"No. The shark never dies. It eats bullets like candy, I think."

I thought of bullets shooting in the shark's mouth, exploding, a snack.

"If we had a gun we could kill it," I said.

"No way," he said. "I can't use guns. I can't or I'll get walloped."

Walloped?

"What's that?"

"Like this—"

Dickens slapped his chin, twice, striking himself so hard the second time that he nearly lost his balance. Then his skin turned bright pink, burning with the imprint of his fingers, and he rubbed his chin, frowning.

"I got walloped plenty," I told him. "At least a thousand."

"Me too," he said. "It's big business, my sister says. She only does it when I'm wrong—which is a lot, I guess."

Dell hit Dickens. She was a walloper, like my mother.

"You miserable creep," I heard her telling him. "What good are you? Explain that to me. I never liked you, I never did, you know."

And there was Dickens—hugging himself, cowering in a corner of their house—talking in his spooked voice, "I'm sorry, I'm sorry, don't—"

He took my hand.

"We better go. Monster shark catches us here and we're doomed. We better hide."

Off we went again; Dickens leading the way, me wondering if he massaged Dell's legs at night. All I could think of was flesh being grabbed and pressed–and an arm raised, ready to swing, poised for the slightest of transgressions.

"Bad dog!"

That's what my mother often said, what she'd call me; sometimes she was joking, mostly she was serious.

"Bad dog! Bad dog!"

What had I done now? Massaged too hard? Massaged too soft? Massaged in one place too long?

Resting in bed, she'd shove her fat legs in my direction. I knew when she was about to start kicking; she always snorted, then exhaled an angry breath. And I could easily dodge her feet. I was fast. Her legs operated in slow motion. But her hands were another story.

"You're a bad dog," I admonished Dickens, who'd just returned from using the bathroom in the Johnsongrass. "You watered all the fish and seaweeds."

"No," he said, shaking his head, "you're the bad dog!"

We were sitting inside Lisa.

Or Lisa II, as Dickens now referred to the repaired wigwam; he'd patched the fallen roof, removed the tires and bicycle. On her maiden voyage, we explored the ocean floor together, hoping for an encounter with the shark–but, as evening approached, we grew tired of the search and surfaced.

"What can we play?"

"I'll think."

Late afternoon light streamed through the cracks in the submarine, shining on us, illuminating the scant hairs sprouting from Dickens' nipples. He patted his narrow rib cage; his chest, smooth and fallow, almost appeared translucent.

"Let's go to the bus," I said. "It's the best place for watching light bugs. They visit me there."

"Can't do that."

"How come? We can play."

"Can't go there."

Dickens paused. He looked at his belly button.

"Take the bus for shark bait and drive it on the tracks and it tips over and burns up–then you get in trouble. Then you can't ever go there again, ever."

He glanced at me, gravely. His toes fidgeted in the flip-flops.

"And I'm not supposed to drive anyway, you know. Or steal buses, or steal anything anymore. That's what gets me in all the trouble–even if it was a million years ago. Lucky they didn't send me away forever, all right? Lucky I didn't burn and die too. And Sheriff Waller said you have to have a license–and even then you can't take a bus–'cause it isn't the same as Daddy's tractor either. You can't drive a bus on the tracks or it tips and burns, you should know that. That'll get you sent away, Dickens, so I can't go there with you."

"Oh," I said, confused.

Captain, you're acting silly, I thought. You're crazy.

He mumbled, "Sometimes you just worry about it too much–just pretend it never happened, okay?"

"Okay," I replied, uncertain if he was talking to me or himself.

Then he was standing, saying, "I better go home now and eat, I think. We shouldn't play no more today."

It didn't matter. I was bored with playing. My stomach ached for crackers and bread.

"But you have to save my friend, you said you'd do that."

"I don't know how," he said. "I make mistakes if I try some things."

"I'll show you," I told him. "You promised."

And then it was me taking his hand; I wasn't planning on releasing my grip–not until he squatted at the hole, not until he used his hand to rescue Classique.

"But–"

"No, you have to," I said, tugging at his arm.

Soon I walked alongside the embankment with Dickens in tow. Already my head swam, my stomach burbled, a mixture of anticipation and hunger. We passed by Dell's meadow of bluebonnets and rocks. Then we wandered across the clearing of threshed grain–clomping on white stalks that had turned golden in the evening rays–and headed for the shaded footpath, where mesquite branches crisscrossed overhead. Behind me Dickens' feet flip-flopped.

And when we arrived at the hole, I loosened my hold on his hand and explained that Classique had fallen from my finger: "But she's pretty close. But my arms aren't like yours and I can't get her, but you can. She's really close. It isn't very far, it just looks far in there."

Dickens knelt. He stared at the hole, pondering the darkness within.

"What is your friend?" he asked.

"A head. A Barbie head."

"Does she bite?"

"No. Her mouth is like this–"

I pressed my lips together for a moment.

"She doesn't have teeth."

"All right," he said, nodding.

Then his arm sank inside the hole, slowly, all the way to his shoulder. He brought out both parts of the broken branch and tossed them aside–he slid his arm in again. Then out.

A handful of dirt and pebbles.

In again.

And his face strained as he felt around. My heart began racing.

"Don't know," he said. "Just can't find nothing."

I was on my knees, beside him, watching.

"Wait. I got her. It has to be her. It has to be–"

Out.

An oblong stone, bigger than Classique, sat in Dickens' palm.

"She's weird," he said. "Not a head at all, not like you said."

I was suddenly tired and dizzy. I lifted the stone and let it drop to the ground.

"No," I said. "No, no–"

"That's all that's down there," he told me. "Nothing else, okay? Nothing but dirt and more dirt."

"She's dead," I said.

In the distance, the train whistle blew. Dickens glanced in the direction of the tracks.

"Uh-oh, the monster shark—it's coming."

Then he made the erupting noise with his mouth.

But everything was spinning, so I shut my eyes. My body became heavy. And I slumped forward. And I don't recall much after that—except sensing my fall. I was entering the hole, tumbling straight into blackness, disappearing. The earth had swallowed me up.

16

What Rocks had drowned.

I stirred on my father's bed–reversed in position, my head resting at the foot of the mattress–disoriented, lightheaded, and parched; everything around me was tinted in ultramarine, blurry. The ceiling. The lamp glowing at the center of the night table. My dress, my legs, my sneakers. The backpack and small pile of dirty clothes and the Peach Schnapps bottle, all clumped at my feet. Blue and slightly out of focus.

At the bottom of the sea, I thought.

My fingertips touched my face, feeling for wetness. And I opened my mouth wide, expecting a gush of water, but found myself swallowing air instead. Then I realized the goggles were covering my eyes, the frayed elastic band pressed against my ears.

"And then you fly," Dickens said.

Turning my head sideways, I saw him. He sat on the throw rug, playing with Magic Curl and Fashion Jeans and Cut 'N Style. The heads lounged in his level palm, a flying carpet sailing back and forth above his lap–and he was underwater, breathing as effortlessly as a goldfish.

"We sunk," I rasped.

Dickens glanced at me, his palm stopping in midair.

"No," he said softly, "Dell says you nap until she's done with him. Or she says you stay here and eat something if you wake, all right? You're lucky she's strong and held you–lucky she rescued you or I'd have fainted too."

Dell rescued me.

"Did she suck my blood?"

"She doesn't do that. That's wrong."

"Oh."

My belly groaned.

"I'm hungry," I told him.

"That's what she said," he muttered, returning his attention to the heads. "She already said that."

His palm landed; he lifted each head, one at a time, setting them upright on the rug.

"A safe crater trip–everyone had a safe trip visiting the moon."

Then he climbed from the floor and crossed to the night table. And I propped myself up–pushing the goggles off my eyes, onto my forehead–so I could see what he was doing.

"I'm pretty thirsty."

I squinted; without the goggles, the room seemed unbearably bright.

"Buff-low jerky," he was saying. "Yum. Sometimes I get jerky too–if I'm smart and don't be stupid."

"Dickens, did I fall far?"

"On the ground is all. Plop."

"Oh, I didn't go in the hole."

"No, don't think so. I think I'd remember that, I think."

He came toward me carrying a paper plate and a Dixie cup.

"There's more later," he said, handing me the cup, putting the plate down on the mattress.

"Thank you," I said, bringing the cup to my lips, "thank you–"

Warm apple juice–pouring over my tongue, sweet in my throat–I drank it in two big gulps. And the jerky, four round pieces, brown shriveled chunks, tough as a toenail; I ripped the dried meat between my teeth, milling with my jaw, chewing like a fiend.

"See, if you chomp fast you'll choke."

Dickens made a gagging noise.

"That happens sometimes and you can't breathe."

He stood nearby, watching while I ate, following the jerky as it went from the plate to my teeth.

"Tastes good, I bet," he said. "Smells awfully good."

I would've offered him some, but there wasn't enough. Besides, I was starving; my stomach had become a deflated balloon.

"It's buff-low," he was telling me. "They kill them and they create circles so you can keep them in your pocket—"

"Dickens!"

Dell hollered from downstairs.

"Dickens!" she shouted.

Her voice recalled my father's baritone grumble, and my lips parted with amazement, my jaw froze. I stared at Dickens, who, upon hearing her, studied the floor as if it were made of glass.

"She needs me."

His gape met mine. He frowned.

"I'd like my glasses again, please—'cause I was only trading when I played with your toys, okay? But I'm not playing anymore, so I don't have to be fair now."

"I don't care," I said, talking with a mouthful of jerky.

I removed the goggles and dangled the elastic band from my fingers.

"Okay," he said, taking the goggles, "you stay here, all right? She says you should. She's in a mood, I think."

I shrugged.

"Dickens! Dickens!"

"Uh-oh."

He jumped, swung about-face, and flip-flopped away. I listened as he thudded down the stairs.

"I'm sorry," he mumbled, "I'm sorry—"

Then silence. I couldn't hear anything else.

And suddenly What Rocks existed somewhere on the moon, enveloped by a crater, lost. The darkness outside confirmed this notion. So I finished eating, pondering the fate of the farmhouse-spaceship. Dell and Dickens and my father were in the living room and plotting our survival. And I was lucky to be alive, lucky that Dell could help me, thankful for buff-low jerky and apple juice.

But Classique—

"Poor Classique."

Perhaps she'd fallen so far and so fast that her head incandesced like a meteor. With a brave face, I explained her sad fate to the other heads. But only Cut 'N Style was upset—she cried gallons of tears, until a pool formed beneath her, soaking the throw rug and seeping into the hem of my dress.

"She just disappeared," I told Cut 'N Style, "so don't cry. She didn't feel any pain, I'm sure."

But my words weren't helpful; Cut 'N Style was inconsolable. I held her to a cheek, trembling, while Magic Curl and Fashion Jeans gloated.

"You'll get walloped," I warned them. "If Classique was here, she'd destroy you both."

And I wished Classique had been there that night, accompanying me as I tiptoed from the bedroom. I wish she'd floated downstairs, going where my father's stink lingered with the persistent aroma of disinfectant. She might've understood what I spied when gazing into the living room—all the furniture moved against the wall, the entire floor blanketed by an orange plastic tarp; my father stretched naked there, on his back, with discolored patches, black and purple, showing everywhere—abdomen, chest, thighs—and blisters spread across his legs and feet, like welts, making a spiral pattern on his bloated tummy. His jeans and boots and boxers and socks and shirt—his sunglasses and the wig and the bonnet—were heaped in the leather chair. His ponytail was loosened, his mane of hair flowed out on the tarp, as if the wind had just swept over him. And the lipstick and rouge—gone; his cheeks now swabbed clean and completely white. In fact–aside from the blisters and discolored patches–he was pale, drained; a gash smiled under his chin, crossing his neck–a fresh slit, pink and thin and tender, grinning while he slept; his features relaxed, his eyelids shut.

But what was in the buckets?

Eight large containers, placed around the body. The one nearest his head, full and murky; my father's rotten blood, thick as molasses and sanguine, almost reaching the rim– some on the tarp, drops spattered here and there.

And why the bail of wire? The tacks? The brushes? The saw and claw-hammer? The scissors? The scalpel? The paring knife? And all that cotton batting? And the assorted needles? The ball of twine? The box of borax and the paper towels and the cans of Lysol and the rubber gloves–and the dozen or so odd-shaped canisters and bottles?

Was anything forgotten?

"Wrong, child, who welcomed you down here?"

"Not me, Dell, I didn't–"

The living room wasn't the living room; it'd become an operating theater. And Dell was surgeon. And Dickens the nurse.

And my father–

"So much damage already. But I'll save what's left, right? He'll never be the same, poor man."

There I stood beside the wood-burning stove, uncomprehending, a rag doll unable to speak.

"Yes, Rose, wigs and blush won't cut it, child. You're a baby, yes, yes. And now you've stumbled upon my calling, of course. So stay put and watch if you must–but know this–be quiet or else. I can only do so much, right? Audiences and peeping toms make me a nervous nelly. This isn't fun, sad man–sad sad man."

Her calling required dishwashing gloves and the scalpel, but not the hood and helmet. She'd gathered her hair into a bun, had donned fishing waders that were mostly concealed underneath her housedress. And how familiar she was with my father, straddling him, shaking her head, saying, "To meet once more–and like this–what an unfortunate shame. I won't let you go this time, I won't."

She knew him. She knew his name.

"Sad Noah–into my arms again. The Rose child is yours, I suppose. You never told me, no, no." She continued speaking to my father all the while, touching him here and there as she worked, muttering, "There's never been another, Noah. No, no, no, never another, you've known that. I've waited for you these years, so now you're staying put. I'm keeping you–you won't be leaving me anymore. I'm protecting you, right? And the Rose child, she's family now, see? She'll be fine, darling one. But she'll stay here with you, because this is where you belong. And I'm so close, right? I'm just across the tracks. And this way, of course, you won't be going anywhere. Not somewhere else, or in the ground. Strangers won't take you away. You'll stay put for a long while. No more running away." Then she kissed him on the lips. She kissed my father, saying, "I love you so much, dear sweet man–so much–"

And how intimate she was while making an incision along the middle of his belly, cutting up to the center of his breast bone. How handy she was with that razor-sharp scalpel–slicing each of his palms, continuing a little ways along the back of the wrists–then piercing his soles; the scalpel traveling onward, steadily, over the ankles.

"Sinister apples," she uttered when an incision was completed. "Sinister sinister apples."

But those weren't the words Dickens repeated; mumbling as he went outside, gripping the bucket of my father's blood: "I'm tired tired tired–"

And so was I, perhaps. Or possibly shock–not sleep–overtook me during that long night, bowing my head, bringing my body to the floor, drawing my knees in toward my ribs. And if Classique had been there, she could've told me what transpired while I lay unconscious.

Or perhaps I was awake and observed it all–how the tools were used, how the skin was peeled, how the intestines were held. The gristle and tissue cleaned from the nose. The brain spoon made by hammering and shaping a wire tip. The eyeballs snipped from the sockets. The removal of tendons. My father's meat scraped and sheared, dumped into buckets. The fat trimmed from the underside of his skin. The bones sprinkled with powdered borax—and the heavy wire fashioned into strips, bunched into balls. Each bucket now filled and hurried outside. Dickens in the yard—surrounded by buckets, digging the earth with a spade—as sunlight began filtering through the Johnsongrass.

Imagination or memory?

"Sinister apples."

Dell the butcher, rolling my father this way and that on the tarp, sewing him together. Then the smell of varnish, like nail polish, obliterating his stink.

And did I dream? Was it the mystery train rattling at dawn, shaking me where I slept?

"Rise, Rose—"

Dell was nudging me with a wader.

"Rise and behold Noah."

Rise and behold my father, arms at his side, legs straight; glistening, coated with varnish, mended and stitched—except for a rabbit-hole where his navel once budded, strands of wire lurking within. A hole bigger than my fist, cavernous, waiting to be seamed.

"Is he better?" I asked.

"Of course," Dell replied, "of course."

But he didn't look anything like my father. She'd given him a haircut, cropping his hair close to his scalp. His eyelids were sewn shut, bits of twine appearing as overgrown eyelashes. And his skin was lumpy in places, deformed. Still, he didn't seem miserable. The varnish gave him life. He glowed.

"You'll offer him a gift, yes?"

Dell pointed at the hole.

"Something that's dear to you, Rose. Something he can keep by his heart."

"Like what?"

"No, no, you decide. You pick the treasure for the chest."

But what could I offer?

"Wait, I know."

Two heads, the traitors–Magic Curl and Fashion Jeans, both screaming and weeping as I lowered them into the hole.

"Not me! Not me!"

"Please, please, please–"

"Goodbye," I said, letting them drop. "Have a safe trip."

And they wouldn't stop blubbering, even after Dell had sewed up the hole and applied the final coat of varnish. I could hear them, echoing inside my father.

"Help us! Help us!"

"There's no light and we can't breathe!"

Then a funny thing happened, I started crying. Tears surged, splashing from my lashes, streaming along my cheeks. Sobs caught in my throat.

"It's the fumes, of course," Dell said.

She reached out, resting a gloved hand on my shoulder. And when I moved to embrace her, she stepped back, withdrawing her arm.

"It's unhealthy for your lungs, these fumes. Go to the porch and draw in. Go, I say–draw in."

So I trudged outside–brushing dry the tears, stifling the sobs–and breathed on the porch. Only a hint of Lysol and varnish persisted, sneaking through the open door and raised windows. Otherwise, the morning air smelled fresh and cool, like spring water. And at last the sun was ending the dark hours; a reddish hue burned beyond the sorghum, bleeding under the starry sky.

In the yard, Dickens scooped dirt with the spade, wearily replenishing the pit he'd created. The buckets littered the ground, empty and upturned among the weeds. During the night he'd acted as Dell's helper, fetching what tools she asked for, taking what was already used–or wasn't needed– and placing them into one of the four duffel bags on the porch. But now he was spent, pausing between scoops, adjusting his goggles and wiping his brow.

"When he's done, we'll be going."

Dell brought me jerky, three pieces.

"Tonight I'll return," she said. "But I'm tired as sin and my work is accomplished."

I began devouring the jerky while she slipped off the gloves, gnawing and smacking as she tossed the gloves on top of a duffel bag. Then she lifted her glasses and rubbed the bridge of her nose. And I caught a glimpse of her pirate-eye, the milk-white pupil and iris. A dead peeper—that's what my father called a baked trout's eyeball; that's why I didn't eat his trout. I hated those eyes.

Dell lowered the glasses and found me with her good peeper. She jiggled a thumb at the duffel bags.

"They'll remain for the time being. Don't mess with the contents, please."

I nodded, chewing.

"Tonight we'll put your house in order. An untidy home means an untidy person. This is where you belong, this is your place. So you get rest. And leave Noah be—he must dry, understand?"

I imagined my father withered like a chunk of jerky, his skin tightening and growing brown.

"He's a bog man," I said.

"Nonsense, such dribble," Dell replied, and her ferociousness simmered below the surface; her good eye glared and her lips tapered. "Rose, that man is no bogeyman! What a terrible thing to say, horrible!"

She turned—her housedress swishing against my knees—and marched away, shielding her face, protecting herself from a bee attack. I watched as she pounded down the front steps in her waders. And just then I heard the squirrel overhead, scampering on the steel awning. Dell heard him too. She twisted around in the yard, peering between fingers, glowering at the roof. Her hands parted briefly and she spit.

"Nasty—!" she cursed the squirrel.

And the squirrel chattered and ran. He tore over the awning, no doubt heading for his knothole.

Then Dell ambled toward Dickens, who had finished scooping dirt and was stomping on the pit with his flip-flops. And I tried not to think about what had slid from the buckets, what was now buried there in the yard. I wanted to eat and not think about anything.

But my brain wouldn't quit.

World full of holes, I thought. Holes everywhere, full of people and things. Squirrels and doll heads and bog men. Things go inside holes and sometimes never come out again for a thousand years. Some houses are like holes too, like tombs.

I ripped at the jerky, picturing this mummy that was once on TV. He was in Egypt. He was a king. Several of the men who discovered him died mysteriously. One choked on his vomit, another was smashed by a slab of marble. The TV voice said mummies had strange powers.

Dell and Dickens wandered toward the cattle trail, disappearing among the high grass. And I swallowed, wondering if my father had any powers, if it would take all day for him to dry.

17

Like an airship descending–the picnic basket landed beside the wood-burning stove, the silverware clanked, and Dell said, pulling back the top, removing a foil-covered plate from within, as if she were proffering a cargo of rare jewels, "For the Rose child of dear Noah–"

Beer-Braised Rabbit, she explained, with carrots and onions and potatoes. A thermos of apple juice. Pound cake for desert, one slice.

"A very special treat."

She'd returned after nightfall, hoodless and without Dickens, in unusually cheerful spirits, bringing the basket and the plaid quilt.

"We've chores ahead," she told me, "so eat. Stuff yourself."

It was an indoor picnic, and I was the guest of honor–swigging from the thermos, alternating bites of rabbit with bites of cake–watching as Dell wrapped my father in the tarp, bundling him like a mummy. Then she rolled him up in the quilt until only his head was exposed, and used safety pins to join the fabric and bind the untucked corners.

"Looks like a burrito," I said.

"Ridiculous. Don't speak with food in your mouth, you'll choke."

When I was done eating, we straightened the furniture in the living room, and folded my father's clothes, stacking them neatly on the leather chair. Then Dell asked about the map dropping from the wall.

"It's Jutland," I said, "or Denmark, I'm not sure."

"And why does it exist here?"

I shrugged.

"We're supposed to be in Jutland instead of Texas. It's his favorite place to live. But I guess we got lost or something, I guess."

"Rose, I don't understand what you're saying."

She yanked the map from the wall, squinted her good eye, and studied Denmark closely.

"What a strange secret," she finally said, looking at my father, addressing him. "I knew you so well and you never told me. No, this isn't right, no."

A frown crossed her face as she crimped the map into a compact square, creasing the edges. Then Denmark vanished in a pocket of her housedress. She patted the pocket twice, glancing at me.

"Enough of that nonsense," she said. "Your house must be ordered. There's too much filth, of course. We must clean clean clean."

And that's what we did.

In a duffel bag on the porch, there was a feather duster and a no-wax cleaning spray and plastic trash sacks and a sponge. Grandmother had a broom and dustpan in the kitchen. So my job was sweeping. Dell dusted. We started downstairs, in the living room, and worked our way upstairs, sweeping and dusting, collecting grime, making gray and fuzzy piles as we went. She whistled, blowing her pretty song, dancing the feather duster across windowsills, across the dining room table and the oak sideboard. I listened to her song, humming it to myself, while gathering dead June bugs and dirt balls, while dustpanning cracker crumbs and army ant bodies. And soon the air became rich with particles. My nostrils tingled, and both Dell and I sneezed from time to time.

"Mold gets in your head, makes you sick."

We were in the kitchen. Dell dropped the remaining slices of Wonder Bread into a trash sack.

"Crackers are stale, no good, probably sampled by mice."

Into the trash sack.

"But you won't want for food," she said. "Dickens will bring your supper."

Then she wiped down the counter and sink. She cleaned peanut butter off the peanut butter jar, dumped water from the gallon water jugs.

"Bad water is poison."

"What can I drink then?"

She set the jugs on the floor.

"I'll fill them at home and have Dickens bring them 'round tomorrow. See, Rose, we'll care for you, right? We share Noah now. He's ours and you're his. You brought him back to me, I think. You understand, correct? You're part of the family now—and this is where you belong, right? So we can't have strangers, of course. If they come, they'll take your father from both of us. It's very simple—strangers always create messes, and messes mean problems. But I fix things, child. I stop Death from proceeding, and I keep troublesome strangers away—that's my calling. How do I say this so you'll understand everything? When it comes to the things we treasure, child, nothing has to die or go into the ground. When you love something, everything can almost stay the same, correct? Then I don't have to be alone, neither do you. Am I making sense? So this is what I do—I keep strangers and Death away so nothing has to change—not Mother, not dear Noah, not this house, or my house, or even you or me or Dickens. I tidy problems as I hold up a hand to Death and shoo him off like a filthy fly—that's what a caretaker for silent souls does. Am I making myself clear?"

"I think so," I said. "You don't want him to be in Denmark."

"Nonsense," she replied. "I don't know what you're talking about. What does Denmark have to do with anything. Don't be silly, silly child. You haven't been listening to a word I've said. Pay attention next time."

I didn't know what to say, so I just stood there gripping the broom handle, looking at Dell's black lens.

"Don't gawk," she said. "We're burning moonlight. There's more to do, there's always more to do."

Upstairs—sweeping and dusting, swabbing the toilet and the bathtub, clearing spiderwebs from the ceiling. In my father's bedroom, folding his dirty clothes and zipping them inside his backpack, dumping the Peach Schnapps' bottle and plastic baggy in a trash sack.

"What's happening?" Cut 'N Style wondered as I lifted her from the throw rug, placing her on the night table.

"We're getting clean clean clean," I told her.

In my bedroom—humming Dell's song—taking the doll arms and the legs and the torso from the mattress, putting them in my suitcase.

And my mother's satin nightgown—

"Good lord, child, what's this?"

Dell held the gown up by its arms.

"It's my pajamas," I said.

"No, no," she said, "it's too large for you. I think so. I think you'll have to wait until you're a woman—and a big one at that."

Then, grinning as if she'd just found a great bargain, Dell took the gown downstairs—where I spied it later in the picnic basket, packed beside the thermos and silverware and crumpled foil and greasy plate.

"Hard workers deserve gifts," she said.

So she got the gown, I got another piece of pound cake—and at dawn, once our work was completed, once all the trash and cleaning material had been crammed into the duffel bags, we moved my father upstairs. Or Dell did. She dragged him across the floor, bumped him up the stairs, and then carried him to my bedroom—not his—resting him on my mattress.

"The sleep of the just," she said. And she kissed his varnished forehead. And I did too.

We sat on the edge of the mattress—Dell by my father's head, me by his wrapped feet—saying nothing for a while. She sighed deeply, whistled for a moment, and then asked if I knew my grandmother.

"No. She died when I wasn't even born yet."

"I see," she said. "Well, you missed a saint. She tended my sorry body after that bee nearly killed me dead. I owe her my life."

"Oh," I said.

That's why you're scared of bees, I thought. That's why you have the hood.

"How come you don't wear the hood anymore?"

And she explained that bees swarmed by day, slept at night.

"Busy beasts," she said. "Buzzy beee-stssss!" she hissed.

She removed her glasses, showing me her pirate-eye. I leaned forward, spotting my reflection on the milky pupil.

"Stung in my own garden," she said. "Blinded by a filthy bee. Revenge, I say, for destroying Father's hives. Poured gas on them all, set them ablaze at midnight."

"Why'd you do that?"

"Ah, well, Father loved his bees, you know. And his bees loved him, I'm sure. Jealous creatures though. Hated Mother. Attacked her in the kitchen. Swarmed through the window. Made her a pin cushion, poor dear. Little stingers dotting her head. Did you know a bee tried crawling up her nose? Pure evil. So Mother's heart stopped and she never finished the dishes. I found her there in the kitchen. Pumped her chest and got her going again. But she wasn't the same, no, no. Couldn't leave her bed. And Father went away—guilt and misery, I tell myself—forever disowning me and Dickens and Mother—and his hives. So I set them ablaze, Rose, in the middle of the night. And now there isn't a bee alive who wouldn't want me murdered. And this—"

She shut her good eye, leaving the bad one open.

"—this is revenge."

"A dead peeper," I said.

She nodded.

"Dreadful, isn't it? But I see more than most–even with eyes closed. Do you know this? Birds and rabbits–they're in my dreams–and children hiding behind bushes, everything you can imagine. Of course, children behind bushes sometimes see more than they should. It's best minding one's own business, right? Otherwise, Rose, bad bad things might happen under the sun."

She'd seen me and Classique. She knew we saw her sucking Patrick's blood. My face turned bright red. I put my head down. For a second, I considered running, but I didn't know where to go.

"Horrible," Dell was saying, sniffing. "Awful. You reek of the devil, Rose. Come with me."

I followed her to the porch, where she dug a can of Lysol from a duffel bag and had me stand on the steps.

"Seal your mouth and eyes," she said. "Extend your arms and hold your breath."

She sprayed my dress and legs, my arms and hair, my sneakers and back. The Lysol felt sticky on my skin. And when I opened my mouth and inhaled, the disinfectant made me gag and cough.

"Do your panties," she instructed, handing me the can.

And as I raised my dress with one hand, spraying my panties with the other, Dell went to the duffel bags. She wound the drawstrings around her fingers, two bags in her left hand, two bags in her right hand. Then she squatted, preparing to lift–but the squirrel caught her attention. He chattered on the roof, creating a racket.

"Monster!" she shouted. "Nasty thing!"

She upheaved, rising with the bags. The veins in her neck bulged as she trudged toward me.

"I'm going home," she said, straining, "while the bees are still napping. Dickens will fetch the basket tonight. He'll bring you water and food. Tomorrow I'll come for that nasty creature, that diseased brute."

She staggered past me, grunting as she ambled through the yard.

"Bye," I said, waving the Lysol can. "I'll guard your spray. And I really like your cake too."

And the next day, I watched from an upstairs window as Dell readied her ambush. It was like something in a cartoon—twine tied to a stick in the yard, a stick set vertical—propped between the ground and an upturned crate—and the twine coiling away, stretching into the Johnsongrass, where she now waited to spring her trap. And there on a plate, beneath the half-cocked crate, a carrot or an onion or a chunk of wood? I couldn't tell. Then scampering over the roof, along the awning, down into the yard—how long did it take? Longer than a cartoon, I suppose, shorter than Romper Room. The squirrel was careful, not too fast, approaching the crate in furtive darts and sudden stops, sniffing as he crept toward the plate.

"Watch out," I said.

The twine tightened. The stick collapsed. And like a shark engulfing a minnow, the crate swallowed the squirrel in one chomp. But the squirrel fought; he struggled about, almost tipping the crate, resisting so violently that Dell had to run from the Johnsongrass and sit on her trap. She clutched an empty duffel bag, which, eventually, she worked underneath the crate, consuming the trap and the squirrel and the plate. Then she pulled the drawstrings and hoisted her load—the squirrel clawing inside the bag—and hiked to the cattle trail, whistling.

Beer-Braised Squirrel, I thought. That's what she'll cook me. That's what I'll get.

"Poor squirrel," I told my father. "He's doomed. He never had a chance."

18

The hospital was inside my father's belly, a shadowy and grim place smelling of varnish.

"A full recovery is expected," someone said.

And dressed in green johnnies, my mother and Classique lay beside one another on gurneys. Three surgeon Barbies, breathing hard behind white masks, crowded around them with scalpels.

"Fabulous," said Classique—except she wasn't quite Classique. She had a human body, long legs, a blond beehive. "Fantastic, darling, wonderful!"

"Yes, sweety," my mother concurred, "wonderful!"

My mother looked like Dell. She wore a cowboy hat and smoked a cigar.

And I was there too, somewhere.

Just then a Barbie nurse appeared. Magic Curl? Or Fashion Jeans? I can't say for sure. She carried an oversized brain, the size of a turkey, on a silver platter.

"Your dinner is served," said the nurse. "Set the table."

But what I understood her to mean was: "The brain is ready. Bring the patient."

And Classique was suddenly whisked away, blowing kisses as she went, telling me or my mother, "This is it! I've never been so happy! I'm alive!"

"Yes," my mother said, sitting up and exhaling smoke, "yes, yes!" Her johnny burst into flames.

I awoke, sweating. It was afternoon, and sunlight blazed through my bedroom window, spilling over the mattress, warming me and my father. The varnish glistened like perspiration across his forehead. And I was stretched alongside him, pressed against the quilt, yawning.

"Rise and shine," Cut 'N Style said.

I'd fallen asleep with her on my finger. Now she hovered in front of my face.

"Classique is alive," I told her. "She's okay and happy."

"Just a dream," she replied. "Trust me, I know. I was there, dear."

Cut 'N Style sounded different, more like Classique.

She said, "I know everything."

"Stop it," I said. "Don't pretend you're her."

"That's silly. I have no idea what you're talking about—"

I flicked her from my finger, sent her sailing. She flew to the floor, bounced and rolled, and finally slid to the edge of the stairs. She was knocked out before she could start crying.

"It's not just a dream," I said. "You're pretty stupid if you can't see that—even if you're blind too!"

Then I put an ear to the quilt, listening at my father's rib cage, hoping that the operation was well underway, and that the surgeons' voices could be caught. But I heard nothing.

"Magic Curl," I said softly, "Fashion Jeans—it's me, Jeliza-Rose. What's happening in there? You'll tell me, all right?"

I listened some more, hearing only silence.

Everyone's sleeping, I thought. They're still in the dream.

So I tried making myself fall asleep again. I rested my head on the quilt, shut my eyes and began snoring. But it didn't work. I was wide awake.

"It's not fair!"

In frustration, I climbed from the mattress and rushed

after Cut 'N Style. She was unconscious, probably at the hospital with Classique and my mother. I kicked her down the stairs, saying, "That's what you get, you're a bad dog!"

And later, when Dickens arrived with food, I told him, "Cut 'N Style ruined my great dream. She woke me up and now I'll never know."

I was at the dining room table, and he was removing my meal from a paper sack, arranging each item—thermos, foil-covered plate, slice of pound cake in a sandwich bag, fork and knife—neatly before me.

"She's your friend?" he asked. "She fell in the hole and disappeared forever and I can't find her."

"That's Classique," I said, "not Cut 'N Style. Cut 'N Style is on the floor over there—but Classique is in the hospital—I dreamt her—and I saw her with Mom and Mom was burning."

Dickens frowned and shrugged. He didn't understand, so I explained that Classique was no longer a head. She had a woman's body. And she was getting a real brain.

"Bet it costs a million dollars," he said. "I'd like a new brain sometimes—I think a new one is shiny."

"Yeah—and it was a big brain. She was excited and I guess she wasn't a doll anymore."

Dickens pulled the foil off the plate—"She must be pretty" then unscrewed the thermos cap.

"She is. She's beautiful."

He pushed the plate toward me—greasy meat, two legs, a thigh or a breast.

"Dell says eat what you can and hide the leftovers in this—"

He handed me the foil, which I smoothed in my lap as if it were a napkin. Then I sniffed at the meat, "Is it the squirrel?"

"No," he said, shaking his head. "No squirrel. Dell hates those. She won't cook those—she just won't."

"Oh," I said, reaching for the fork, "that's good. I don't think I like squirrel either."

And while eating, I thought about Classique's operation. How was the brain put in? Did it hurt? Did she bleed? Is she different?

Why did she need a brain anyway?

Because it's fabulous, dear. It's fantastic, darling.

"Fabulous," I said, picking at the meat. "Wonderful."

Dickens glanced at me. He was in the living room, holding my father's wig, his fingers combing the coils. Then I watched as he planted the wig on his bald head; the coils sank past his ears and forehead, adorning his shoulders. And—wearing his goggles and swimming trunks and flip-flops, the wig askew—he looked like a crazy woman, half-naked and loathsome.

"I'm pretty pretty," he said.

"You're funny," I told him. "You're weird."

"No, no," he whined, "because I don't want to be weird, okay? I'd like the red lips and then I'll be beautiful."

He needed more than red lips. He needed rouge, maybe mascara.

"All right," I said, "I'll fix your face."

He clapped.

"Yes, if you fix my face I'll be happy."

"I will," I said. "Except I better eat Dell's cake first, better drink all my apple juice."

"And hide the leftovers."

"I know that already."

But there wasn't going to be any leftovers. I ate every piece of meat, chugged the apple juice, consumed the pound cake in three bites. Then I fetched Grandmother's cosmetic bag—my tummy feeling bloated and satiated, my meal swishing around inside, as I sprinted up and back down the stairs.

"Sit still or else you'll make me do it wrong," I told Dickens, who fidgeted while I unzipped the bag. He was cross-legged on the living room floor, spine straight, hands squeezing his knees.

"Won't move a muscle," he said. "Don't have muscles anyway, so I won't move them."

I shushed him, and then emptied the cosmetic bag between us, shaking out the lipsticks and mascara and com-

pacts and tweezers and cotton balls. I arranged the six lipsticks into a row.

"Now, which one?"

Scarlet Surrender or Pink Tango or Hyacinth or Sweet
Vermilion or Chinese Red or Rose Blush.

"That one," he said, pointing at Pink Tango.

"This is best," I said, taking Scarlet Surrender. "Puff
your lips."

He puckered.

"Get ready—"

It was difficult applying the scarlet evenly. Stay in the
lines, I told myself—but my hand moved too fast when doing
his bottom lip, and I smeared lipstick across his chin. His
upper lip went smoother; I only overshot once, reddening the
end of his nose. But that was his fault. He sniffled and my
hand jerked.

"You're Rudolph," I said.

"You are," he replied.

Then I dabbed on the rouge, brightening his cheeks, creating rosy circles.

"Almost finished," I said, shutting the compact.

He was gazing at me, his eyes magnified behind the goggles.
Bug eyes, I thought. Creepy bug eyes.

"I think you're nice," he said.

And as I leaned forward, straightening the wig, he kissed
my lips—a nervous peck, which tickled and made me giggle.

"That's silly," I said, wiping my lips. "You got red on me,
silly kisser."

He glanced at his swimming trunks, embarrassed, and
folded his hands over his crotch.

"The old lady was a silly kisser too," he said. "She kissed
me, but that's when I was little and she was really old.
Sometimes she did this in my mouth—"

He stuck out his tongue and wiggled it.

"—and that was fun. It was a snake, I think, or a goldfish
dancing. She was awfully sweet too. Sometimes I'd be here all
day just kissing with her. She's a nice lady, except she's dead."

I was both delighted and curious to hear him speak of Grandmother.

"She's Daddy's mom," I said. "She never kissed me because I didn't get born yet."

"I think I knew that. I think maybe someone told that to me."

"Dickens, she was your girlfriend–you were her boyfriend."

He took his hands from his crotch and assumed an expression of sorrow.

"No, I was her cutie. Her little cutie. Never been a boyfriend. Don't know what that is, except if I got older I'd be her boyfriend, I suppose. If she didn't die, you know. If she didn't fall down the steps. Think she was coming to kiss me when she falled 'cause I was there in the yard pulling weeds. And I ran away when she did that. But I didn't know what to do. I was just little, you know. I was scared, I guess. She was nice."

"She was old," I told him, envisioning the chest in the attic, the junk stored within. "How old are you?"

A worried, confused look settled on Dickens' face.

"I don't know. I'm not an old man though. Dell says I'm a boy. She says I'm a baby. She says I'll always be a baby 'cause my brain got wired wrong."

You'll buy a new brain, I thought. When you have the world's biggest penny, you'll get the operation.

"You're a little cutie," I said.

He smiled.

"You're a little cutie too."

So I kissed him.

Then he kissed me.

And we were laughing, our lips and teeth red with scarlet.

"Silly kissers."

I was about to kiss him again when the quarry suddenly boomed, rattling the windows.

"Uh-oh."

Dickens creased his brow. He stared at the ceiling for a moment, the blond coils slipping from his shoulders.

"They're exploding the ground," he said. "They dynamite everything so there's no more left. I seen them do it. I go there and see them. It's bigger than firecrackers and bullets."

"I like firecrackers."

"Me too. I really do. So if you want to see the boom hole, you'll see the ocean too, if you want."

I nodded.

"I'll show you, okay?"

He reached for my hand.

"Okay," I said.

Then we kissed.

19

The captain was my boyfriend, my cutie. And I was his Mrs.
Captain, his special one. When he kissed me, my stomach did
somersaults. When I kissed him, I wanted to stand on my
head and sing. I wanted to spin in circles. Even while we
gathered our expeditionary crew—a Barbie arm as his first
lieutenant, Cut 'N Style as my second Mrs. Captain—I
couldn't stop thinking about those scarlet lips, so strange and
exciting, making my belly tingle. Did he feel the same? Were
my lips tingling someplace within him?

"Onward," he said, assuming his brave captain's voice. "That
ocean boom hole is at least four hundred miles from here."

Four hundred miles in less than an hour. More like two
miles, if that. But how far it seemed, how inhospitable. A
desert of bulldozer tracks and chalky silt. No brush. No grass
or bluebonnets. Just dirt and sand.

Soon my dress was dusty. I tasted grit. And Dickens' wig
had gone white. Limestone flour powdered the scarlet on his
lips, the rouge on his cheeks. He wiped dust from the goggles.

"If the wind blows bad and we don't hold hands," he said,
"then we'll be lost and go blind and then we'll fall in the hole

alone or worse. So watch for the wind, okay? It's a tornado
sometimes or a dust devil. So we better be careful. You drop
in this hole and you're a goner for sure. You can't fly, I don't
think. I can't. I tried but I can't. And I can't swim either."

We'd journeyed to the end of the world–having traveled
through Johnsongrass and tall weeds and across dirt roads
and under barbwire, ignoring DANGER and NO TRES-
PASSING signs–going where the cream-colored earth
sheered and staggered downward; mammoth ledges hewed
from the quarried terrain, large enough for a giant to ascend.

And there we lay, at the edge of a high rock cliff, gazing
over the rim and into the quarry–or into the boom hole, as
Dickens labeled it–pondering the murky water that spread
out below us.

"If you fell you'd drop a hundred years until you splashed
in the ocean."

"How far is that?"

"Almost a thousand miles, I think."

The Hundred Year Ocean lined the very depths of this
cliffbound gorge, still and dark beneath the surface.

"But it's a lake," I said. "The ocean goes forever."

"No," Dickens replied, "no, no. 'Cause it's deeper than
any lake, so don't pretend you know, all right?"

Then he explained that old cars and old trucks and all
kinds of junk lurked somewhere underneath the water. And
freshwater jellyfish, about the size of a penny and transparent.
Years ago, he told me, three scuba divers drowned before
they could find their way back to the surface.

"Cause it don't have a bottom," he said. "Never did.
These people go in sometimes and can't get out. That's why I
got a submarine. That way I don't drown at all."

How often had he explored the bottomless ocean in Lisa?
A zillion million times, maybe. And what did he find? A bat-
tered bicycle, some tires, beer cans–pennies? Hidden treasure?

"Just outta space, blue and red stars too. But you can't
breath in space and Lisa is only a submarine, you know. She
can't be a rocketship and a submarine. But if you sink deep

deep deep then you'll reach the moon and much deeper is Mars and deeper than that is God and the baby Jesus, I think."

"But what about the booms? You're lucky Lisa didn't get exploded!"

"They don't boom this anymore," he said.

Then using the Barbie arm as an indicator, Dickens pointed across the quarry toward its farthest cliff–where a solitary cluster of mesquites stretched alongside the brink.

"Past them trees, these men do it there now. They dynamite that new boom hole but it doesn't even have an ocean or any jellyfish."

No sooner had he spoken when a boom erupted, reverberating like a sonorous thunderclap, quaking our perch, jiggling my insides. Dickens shielded his face in the nook of an arm–and I covered my ears, gaping at the far-off mesquites, expecting fiery billows and chunks of debris to be blazing upward beyond the cluster. Instead–as if the mesquites had suddenly splintered apart–I saw a swarm of black birds shoot from the trees, rising into the sky, shrieking; they sailed around like an angry cloud, sweeping in unison, this way and that, eventually returning to their roosts when the boom had died.

I took my hands from my ears, slowly, listening as the birds squalled.

"They're mad," I told Dickens, who was lifting his head. "They were sleeping, I guess. The booms will kill them if they don't leave soon."

And I remembered my father's story, how as a boy he murdered starlings. So did his cousins. So did Grandmother. Everyone in their town murdered starlings.

"Because they shit on everything," my father said, "and they made so much noise. And it was fun as well, I suppose. We got a dime for each bird we caught and killed. Earned nearly five dollars once, and that bought a feast of gum and hardtack back in those days."

The Annual Clatter Pot Round Up it was called.

Men and women and children–fanning out, walking from one end of town to the other–banging spoons against pots and pans and trashcan lids, frightening the starlings. That racket kept the birds in flight, kept them swooping frantically overhead, searching for a quiet place to land, flying until they couldn't fly anymore–then, exhausted, they began plunging. Starlings came tumbling toward the earth, crashing into streets and sidewalks, in yards and on rooftops. And my father and his cousins and Grandmother and everyone else would start using their spoons like hammers.

"The ones that were breathing and trying to fly again," my father said, "we beat the heads flat. Sometimes we just crushed them with our boots, and sometimes the wings were flapping long after the skulls popped."

My mother hated that story. I did too.

"Dickens, my daddy murdered birds. It's mean doing that."

But he wasn't paying attention.

"That was close," he said.

Then he studied the Barbie arm for a while, pressing a thumb into the plastic flesh.

"I got a secret," he finally said.

"What is it?"

"If I say you can't tell, okay? If Dell knows she'll wallop me good and then I'm in trouble forever."

"I got a secret too."

He looked at me.

"Give me your secret and I'll give you mine, okay?"

"Okay."

We both sat up on the cliff, crossing our legs like Indian chiefs. Then I shut Cut 'N Style in a fist so she couldn't hear. And I whispered my secret, saying that he was my boyfriend, that I was Mrs. Captain–and that I liked silly kissing his lips.

"Oh," he said, "mine is different–mine is that I got dynamite in my room and that's bad news for me."

Dynamite. Two sticks. He found them at the new boom hole, he said.

"I forget everything," he said, "and stealing is what gets

me in trouble. That's what happens, that's why it's a secret."

"I'd like to see," I said.

He sighed, drawing his mouth into a tight circle.

"I don't know, maybe tomorrow when Dell drives to town. I don't know. When she drives to town I'm in charge, so I can take care of myself if I want."

"If you show me I'll believe you," I said. "If you show me, you can keep the arm as my birthday present."

He was supposed to smile, but his face revealed nothing. He glanced at the arm.

"What's its name?"

"Army," I said.

"Is it a boy or a girl? A girl is nice, I think."

"It's a boy."

"How can you tell?"

I took the arm and held it between my legs, aiming the diminutive appendage outward as if it were a boy thingy.

"That doesn't mean it's a boy," he said.

"Yes it does. It's a thingy. You got a thingy, I know."

"No."

"I can see it after we peck. I can see it bigger."

"No you can't. That's wrong. I don't have that."

He rocked forward, folding his forearms over the front of his trunks. A soft breeze pushed around us, stirring the dust in the wig, powdering us with rock flour.

I set the arm on his left knee.

"Dickens, I'd like to see your dynamite."

"Maybe tomorrow," he said, "when Dell goes to town. I don't know."

"But you're my boyfriend," I said.

"I don't understand that," he replied, removing the wig, dumping it in my lap. "I better get home, I think."

I love you, I thought. You are my dear sweet captain.

And on the cliff high above the Hundred Year Ocean we kissed for a moment in the late afternoon, then we wandered away, silently, listening as we went, hoping for another boom that never came.

20

Cut 'N Style wouldn't shut up.

"Dickens has a girlfriend," she teased. "He's your boyfriend."

"He's my husband," I told her. "I'm his wife."

"He's a dreamboat. He's a sunny cloud."

It was morning, hours before noon. And even though Dickens always brought my meal after lunchtime, I waited on the porch steps for his arrival.

"Kiss me," Cut 'N Style said.

"That's gross. You're a girl."

"Please. Kiss me and I'll be a boy."

"Girls don't kiss girls that way."

"Please–"

I kissed her, but it wasn't the same as kissing Dickens; there wasn't any tingling in my belly. Then I consumed her with my mouth, sucking her from my finger, pretending that she was a trout and I was a whale. Her skin tasted like soap, her hair like licorice. She made me gag. So I spit her into my palm.

"You're disgusting," I said.

And she was supposed to cry or complain. Instead she started laughing.

"That was fun," she said. "That was great."

You're nuts, I thought. You're crazier than the wind.

Then we were both laughing.

"You're my best friend," I told her.

"And you're mine too."

"And I love Dickens."

"He's the sweet prince. He's the great king."

"He's apple juice and jerky."

"We're a happy family."

"That's what we are."

And Dell would take care of us all. Soon she'd watch our babies while we explored the Hundred Year Ocean. She'd marry my father and become my mother. Then she and Dickens and Cut 'N Style and I would build a castle from mesquite branches and flattened pennies. We'd eat meat and pound cake at every meal. We'd drink juice from gold-plated Dixie cups.

"It's a dream come true," I said.

"It's Christmas," Cut 'N Style said.

My belly tingled. I poked my stomach, imagining a baby squirming within, a Barbie baby with real rooted eyelashes and blue goggles and a real brain. I saw it on TV—if a boyfriend silly kissed a girlfriend enough times, something was bound to happen.

"Tell Dickens," Cut 'N Style was saying. "Tell him about the castle and the babies. And then you'll see his dynamite. Maybe Dell is driving to town already and he's there alone thinking he'd like you to visit and see his dynamite."

"But maybe she's still there—"

"And she'll invite us for a tea party or picnic because she loves Daddy and she's our friend too. That's why she won't drink our blood. Anyway, she doesn't do that anymore, Dickens said so."

My stomach grumbled; the baby was kicking around. That's why my belly always tingled while Dickens and I squished our lips together–every peck caused the baby to grow a little more. I should have known.

"Better tell Dickens," I said. "I think a baby is in me from kissing. I think it's Classique, I think. She's coming back."

"Let's go tell," Cut 'N Style said. "Let's touch the dynamite."

And as we drifted from the steps, a shiver shot through me, beginning at the base of my neck and rippling down my spine. I pictured Dell and Dickens' dark house–the windows locked, the shades shutting out the daylight–their bee-stung mother dozing somewhere inside.

A castle is safer than a home or a farmhouse, I thought. A castle keeps bees and ants from attacking everyone.

When we arrived, their house seemed as unknowable and forsaken as ever. On either side of the gravel walkway, the beds that once fostered tomatoes and squash were now barren, just upturned soil and withering vines. The dirt yard was littered with bootprints and twigs. And moving onto the porch, I noticed that the yellow floodlight no longer glowed above the front door; the imagined queen mother of all fireflies was defunct.

I knocked–quietly at first, three soft raps with my knuckles.

"Hello," I said, addressing the door. "It's me."

I paused, expecting Dell or Dickens to answer. But neither came.

"It's Jeliza-Rose."

I knocked harder–knock knock knock–then paused again.

"It's really a nice day for a tea party so me and Cut 'N Style are here in case you're not too busy."

I put an ear against the door, held my breath, and listened; nothing–not a creak or a bump or the clomp of flip-flops.

"Maybe they're sleeping," I told Cut 'N Style. "Maybe they're in town."

Maybe they're hiding, she thought. Maybe they're at What Rocks looking for us.

"Maybe."

After that, we tramped from the porch and went alongside the house. And ignoring the sudden pangs in my stomach, I skipped toward the backyard, heading where the weeds and foxtails thrived, where the Ford pickup with the cracked windshield sat. But the Ford was gone.

Stopping near the house, I stood between the curvy ruts left by the pickup's tires, and spotted Dickens–out of his captain's uniform, dressed like a farmer–unlocking the padlock on the storage shed door.

Tell him, Cut 'N Style was thinking. Tell him you've got a baby and he'll show you his secret. He said he would.

Dickens pushed the door open and entered the shed. So I hurried across the backyard, running over the beaten trail, hoping to surprise him. I wanted to tell him that I loved him so much and that Classique was coming back as my Barbie baby. I planned on surprising him with Sweet prince, Classique is on her way; and those words would've sailed past the shed doorway had I not seen the squirrel–if I hadn't hesitated before the shady doorway, gazing to my right at a wooden hutch, puzzled by the tufts of gray fur bulging through the chicken wire, the puffy tail curling in on itself.

Was he dead? No. Asleep? No. Wide awake–lying still with his paws on his muzzle, breathing deeply, watching me with black eyes. See what she s done to me, Jeliza-Rose. See what happens when you re small and hungry all the time. You get trapped and stuck in a cage. I m a prisoner. I m doomed.

I felt sad for him. He wasn't a monster or a nasty thing, only a squirrel, and now he didn't seem so mean. But I didn't dare stick my fingers in the hutch to pet him; if I did, he might bite me. He might confuse me for Dell and chomp my fingers off.

Know what she ll do to me? Go in the shed and you ll understand. Look for yourself. That s right, go on–

And what did I find when stepping beyond the doorway?

A long folding table and wide shelves, each surface crammed with Dell's handiwork, novelties and what-nots, some finished, some in progress. On and around the table—lamps with deer antlers for a base, an antler hat rack, foot stools (the legs formed by two pairs of antlers), deer foot lamps, a dozen or so deer foot thermometers. But it was the shelves that held my attention—a fierce-looking tabby cat ready to pounce on a coiled rattlesnake, squirrels clutching acorns, three rabbits huddled together, a raccoon with a trout in its paws, another tabby biting into the head of a bat, an upside-down armadillo, a convincing jackalope sitting upright; all glassy-eyed creatures, inanimate and posed, mounted like trophies on varnished flat cuts of wood. This was where Dell kept Death at bay, where she saved silent souls from going into the ground. But I didn't want to end up like those creatures—frozen and on a shelf; I didn't want to be stuck like that forever. Might as well go into the ground, I thought. If you can't run around and yell and cut muffins, you might as well be dead.

And there was Dickens, in a corner, his backside to me, unloading a duffel bag, removing paper towels and rubber gloves.

"It's a zoo room," I said.

Upon hearing my voice, his body rigored and he shrieked—dropping the paper towels and gloves, turning sharply with a hand clamped to his mouth; the shrill continued, passing his fingers, filling the shed. So terrifying and startling was his scream that I began yelling too. And for a moment the two of us faced one another, bellowing as if we were being murdered, until the air escaped our lungs.

Then he slumped down on the duffel bag, breathless and hugging himself. My hands trembled. Cut 'N Style quivered on my finger. Outside the squirrel was chattering in the hutch, no doubt aroused by our screams.

"Not fair," Dickens was saying, "not fair."

"You scared me good," I said.

"No, you did that to me, you did. That's not fair."

He was rocking, staring at his boots, mumbling something.

"But it was an accident," I told him. "I just saw this zoo

and I was coming to tell you the news but the zoo made me forget everything and I was wondering if they're dead—they're froze and napping, I guess. I guess that's why we got scared because they're pretty spooky like that."

Dickens head came up, his eyes glaring, as he exclaimed, "That's not right 'cause Dell makes them alive again. That's what she does. And people are so happy they bring old dead dogs and old dead kitties and she's Jesus how she makes them alive. And she does those—" He thrust out a hand, pointing at the lamps and foot stools and thermometers on the table. "And that's what she sells in town when she goes to town. She's an artist—she says so—and a healer." He nodded at the shelved animals. "And they're not spooky, they're friends—and you scared me and that's not fair. I think I fainted."

"I'm sorry," I said, crossing to where he sat.

"Don't do that again or I'll die, okay?"

"Okay."

I hugged him, wrapping my arms about his shoulders, patting his neck with Cut 'N Style.

"I think I'm sorry too," he said. "I think so."

Tell him, Cut 'N Style thought. Tell him.

And with my lips near his ear, I mentioned the baby. I said that he was my husband now, and that Classique would appear soon; she'd be our Barbie baby.

"We can build a castle, and Dell can marry my daddy. But you have to show me your dynamite first."

He went rigid.

"I don't know. That baby sounds like a strange thing—and I can't build a castle. I don't know how, I don't know."

So I whispered, "If you show me your secret, I'll love you forever."

He leaned his head against mine. Our cheeks brushed.

"I'll show you," he said. "Just once only. Except not yet 'cause I need to unpack this bag before Dell gets in. Then I'll show you my room in Momma's house, okay? But if I can't unpack this bag I won't eat tonight. So you wait, okay? But don't touch nothing. You're not supposed to be in here. This place is Dell's place."

"All right," I said, withdrawing myself, "I'll wait for my cutie. You're my kisser."

Then I watched him slowly rise, turn, and bend over the bag. His movements were sluggish and clumsy, his awkwardness suggesting a lack of coordination, his boot heels veering outward from the tips. And after a while I got bored and snuck outside, creeping below Dell's creatures on my way, mindful of the rattlesnake poised to strike.

Going from the shed, the sunlight blinded me; I squinted before the hutches, putting a hand above my eyes.

I m a prisoner.

The squirrel was chattering. He paced nervously, regarding me with surreptitious looks.

"Dell will freeze you alive," I said. "You could eat a bat or a fish."

But she ll have to kill me then she ll freeze me alive. I m not old dead dogs and old dead kitties. I m a hungry squirrel.

"We'll help you," Cut 'N Style said.

His hutch had a little gate which was kept closed by a hook latch.

"You do it," I told her. "I don't want to get in trouble."

But Cut 'N Style wasn't worried. She flicked the hook without thinking twice.

"You're free."

I might have opened the little gate for him and pointed above the weeds and foxtails to the mesquites. It was there, among the trees, that he could flee. I wanted to help him more, but I didn't. Unlatching the gate was enough.

Then I peeked into the shed, making certain Dickens hadn't seen what we'd done. But—with his butt aimed toward the doorway, his hands digging inside the duffel bag—I knew he was unaware. And glancing at the hutch, I saw that the gate now hung open; the prisoner had already slipped away. He was quick, that squirrel. He understood what to do, where to go, how to hide. He wouldn't be tricked or trapped again—and, as the sun warmed my shoulders and arms, I was glad.

21

That day, Dickens and I became ghosts.

As we tiptoed up the back steps, he said, "Can't wake Momma so we can't talk like this 'less it's in my room." His voice dropped to a whisper, "We talk like this first."

"We're quiet ghosts," I said. "Your house is the witch's cave, and we're disappearing and we won't get caught."

He grinned.

"Yes, I think that's right. I think that's a good idea. 'Cause Dell will wallop me for having company."

Then we entered the cave-house—coming into the kitchen, not saying a word, holding hands, the sunlight vanishing with the push and turn of a knob. I felt nearly as blind as Cut 'N Style, but Dickens led the way, tugging gently at my arm. And we floated through darkness, two ghosts, inhaling the familiar mixture of varnish and Lysol, gliding over slippery floorboards, proceeding down a hallway lit only by a cat-shaped night-light.

What's it like? Cut 'N Style wondered.

Halloween, I thought. Black enough for bog men, black enough to fool bees that it's bedtime.

Each door we passed was shut–except one, beyond which I glimpsed the shadowy outline of a mounted game head, an elk perhaps, hanging above a sofa, its massive antlers like branches, bifurcating upward and almost touching the ceiling.

Dickens pulled me further along, around a corner, away from the night-light. Another hallway? A doorway?

What's it like now?

Don't know. Can't tell.

He let go of my hand. And suddenly I heard a click and an overhead lightbulb flickered on–so bright, so unexpected, stunning my sight for a moment.

"My room," he announced, closing the door.

His room–cramped, untidy, befitting a pack rat. Stacked along a wall were National Geographic magazines, hundreds of them, in five or six precarious piles. The floor was a clutter of T-shirts and socks, underwear and jeans, his flip-flops and swimming suit, Coke cans and plates with dried food, spoons and forks–more National Geographics, the pages spread, a chance collage of deserts, starry skies, constellations, killer whales, ocean sunsets and schooners and coral reefs.

"Sometimes it's messy," he said. "Sometimes things stick to your feet, so you better get on my bed so you don't crush nothing important, okay?"

"Okay."

Tacked over his bed was a map, not Denmark, but somewhere else, somewhere with wide ranges and long valleys, indistinct, very blue and strange. And the bed–where he asked me to sit–just a drooping cot, the sheets a green sleeping bag, the pillow a bunched ski jacket.

"I got treasure," he was saying, on his knees, reaching beneath the cot. "I'm rich sometimes. I discover fortunes."

Then he hauled out a tackle box, setting it in my lap. I watched as he knelt between my legs, unfastening the clasps and lifting the top, revealing his prized booty, mostly small things. A gold cuff link, his blue goggles, Army the arm, a bulging Christmas stocking.

And pennies–maybe a thousand, or a zillion?

"Fifty-four. That's almost a hundred, I think. Look at these, I found these somewhere."

A pair of false teeth; I held them, pretending the teeth were biting Cut 'N Style's head.

"Chomp chomp," I said. "Chomp chomp chomp."

Dickens frowned.

"Don't do that," he said. "That's wrong."

Then he took the teeth, exchanging them for the bulky Christmas stocking.

My stomach grumbled.

"Is there candy in it?"

"No, the secret," he told me, shaking the stocking, letting the contents drop to the cot.

"Dynamites," I whispered.

Dynamite, he explained, with time fuses and blasting caps; both sticks weren't really sticks at all—not even red like in cartoons—but slender tan tubes, fashioned from wood pulp or paperboard. In my hands, they felt lighter than rocks.

"How do you boom them?"

"Like firecrackers, I think," he said, his voice rising with excitement. "Like a war bomb!" Then his cheeks puffed and deflated, and he made an exploding noise.

"Kaboom!" I said, tapping a tube with Cut 'N Style's chin.

His palms slid up my legs, scooting under my dress, stopping on my thighs.

"Like the end of the world. But if you use them you can't use them ever again. Then they're worthless junk, just blown to bits. So I'll keep them 'til I'm an old man and then I'll kill that shark with Lisa and be a hero, I'm pretty sure."

"I'll help you. That way we can be on TV."

"'Cause you love me."

"I'm your wife forever."

He laid me back on the cot, where I clutched the dynamite—a tube in each hand—and gazed up at the odd map. And as he pressed an ear to my stomach, his fingers touched my panties.

"That baby's sleeping," he said. "It's snoring."

"She's growing," I told him. "She's coming tonight or tomorrow."

"I bet it's pretty. I bet it's pretty like you."

He was over me now, looking down at my face. But my attention was on the map, on its aquamarine details, the jagged ridges and broad basins.

"Where's that place?" I asked.

"The whole bottom of the sea," he told me.

The whole bottom? I couldn't comprehend it.

He mentioned that the deepest part of the ocean plunged further below the surface than the highest mountain stretched above it. And undiscovered countries existed in the depths, entire cities with people and dogs. There were castles and farms beneath the seas. There were husbands and wives and babies and ghosts.

"And silly kissers too. Kissers that do this—"

He stuck his tongue out and wiggled it at me.

"Yuck."

Then I wiggled my tongue. We'd never kissed like that, but the idea made the tingles begin. Dickens' mouth hovered near my mouth. I raised my head, shutting my eyes, forgetting the map and the dynamite in my fists.

Yuck, Cut 'N Style thought. Yuck.

He thrust against me, gripping my wrists, causing the cot to bump bump bump the wall. And as soon as our tongues met, something crashed on the other side of the wall, seemingly rattled loose by the cot's repeated thumping; I heard it hit the floor and bounce.

My eyes shot open. Dickens' head jerked sideways.

"Uh-oh," he said, his body tensing. "It's Momma, I think."

Then he climbed from the cot, crossing to the door, listening for sounds in the hallway.

"Is she awake?" I asked him.

He turned around, facing me, and the overhead bulb reflected off his scarred scalp. He started to hug himself, but stopped.

"Don't know," he said. "'Cause that never happens but

maybe it happens—so you stay here, okay? If Momma quit dozing I'll go see if she needs soup."

But he didn't move; he just remained at the door, fidgeting, sticking his hands in and out of his pockets.

All of a sudden my heart raced.

"I'm scared," I told him.

"Me too," he said.

I imagined him going and not returning, leaving me trapped alone in the witch's cave.

"If we go together we're safe."

He nodded, saying, "All right, but don't tell Dell you saw Momma. If you promise then you can go."

"I promise."

And before slinking into the hallway like quiet ghosts, I helped Dickens put his treasure away. We hid the dynamite in the stocking. He placed the secret inside the tackle box on top of the false teeth, then shoved the box under the cot and covered it with clothing.

"It's our treasure," I said.

"It's bad news," he said, taking my hand.

After that, we wandered into the hallway, traveling a short distance, entering the adjacent bedroom—where candles flickered on a dressing table, dripping red and white and purple wax onto an enameled plate, casting the room in a muted glow. Dickens wasn't holding my hand anymore. He had left me at the table, had gone forward, vanishing. Then a lamp came on—and there he was, standing by a four-poster bed, peering at the dozer who lay on the sheets.

Momma.

"Dell says someday Momma will wake," Dickens whispered. "She says someday there'll be a pill or a story or something that all you have to do is give it or say it and she'll open her eyes again. Except it will be a long time, so until then Momma stays like this. It's better that way. Because if she gets buried or anything then she's gone for good. So I hope that pill or story gets made pretty soon."

Aside from being smaller, she appeared the same as my

father, wrapped in a wool blanket like a mummy, reeking of varnish, her silver hair cropped. I couldn't quite make out her face—not from where I stood—and that was fine; the bees had used her for a pin cushion—they'd stung her cheeks and nose and eyelids. But now she was sleeping. She hadn't stirred, hadn't heard or created the crash.

Dickens glanced at me and shrugged.

What had fallen? What hit and bounced, keeping my husband's tongue from my mouth? What gleamed when I searched the pitchy floorboards? A baseball. I went for it and picked it up, noticing a pallet alongside the bed, fashioned from quilts—and my mother's nightgown, folded into a square, sitting on a pillow.

Dell's napping spot, I thought. She guards Momma from bees.

"That's not your toy," Dickens whispered.

He was beside me, lifting the baseball from my hand.

"You can't play with it."

Then he turned and stepped to the dressing table. I followed, watching as he carefully set the baseball behind the plate. And what the candles obscured, Momma's bedside lamp illuminated, if only faintly—the dressing table was a shrine, an altar of photographs and keepsakes. Among the candles were necklaces, a briar pipe, marbles, a crystal fish, my father's map of Denmark, a Prince Albert tobacco tin, a silver tray with lipsticks and powders and brushes.

And there, below the mirror, the dead radio.

"That's my gift."

"No, that's Dell's," he said, "that's hers."

I was too busy studying the shrine to argue.

Lining the mirror were black-and-white snapshots, family portraits, abstracted faces from the past—a man and a woman reclining in a porch swing with babies on their knees, a boy hoisting a kite, a girl wearing a hula; those images mixed with pictures of John F. Kennedy and Chekov from Star Trek and Davy Jones from The Monkees and a life-like Jesus carrying his cross—and my father in his heyday, his guitar slung behind a shoulder, a finger pointing at the camera.

In fact, my father was everywhere. Driving a convertible. Eating a hot dog. Signing autographs. Swigging beer in a white T-shirt. Playing pinball. And who was that with him? That girl with her arm around his leather jacket, or kissing his cheek, or mussing his hair. That girl, in every shot, with blond hair and thick lips. Her mouth to his mouth, her fingers in his jacket or under his T-shirt.

Even without sight Cut 'N Style knew.

It's Dell, she thought. She was beautiful once, not fat or a pirate. She loved your daddy. She had two good eyes.

Then Dickens and I were all whispers.

"They were kissers," I said.

"I think so," he replied. "That was forever ago, I guess. But Dell is pretty. That was her boyfriend, that was her special friend. He took care of her for a long time."

"It's my daddy."

"No, I'm not sure. No. Your daddy doesn't look like that boy. I think I'd remember that."

"But it's him and that's Dell—and they kiss. They do it like we do it."

Just then I wanted to be kissed. I wanted his tongue wiggling in me. And I told him so.

"I do too," he said.

My belly tingled.

He took a lipstick from the silver tray and led me to the pallet—where we sat facing one another, our heads ducked so we couldn't see Momma, so she wouldn't see us if she miraculously awoke. And we put lipstick on each other, making our lips red and sloppy. Then we kissed, squishing tongues with closed eyes. His fingers found my panties, and he was tickling me down there. But I didn't care—because I was Dell and he was my father—and we were married and our baby was coming. When we kissed I felt warm and safe, everything inside me crackled like a sparkler; that feeling would continue from now on, I was certain. It would never end.

But it did end, fizzling abruptly with, "Filthy filth! Evil!"

There was Dell, glowering at us with a menacing scowl, grasping her hooded helmet. Before either of us had a chance to start or speak, she nudged Dickens with a boot, pushing him away from me. And what happened next stifled my breath; she pounded the helmet with a fist, a muffled whapping, which sent Dickens scrambling backwards across the floor, against a wall.

"No, Dell, no, no—"

"Rotten! Rotten!"

She threw the helmet down—and it spun from the hood, rolling like a tire on its brim toward Dickens, bumping the wall near his right knee, missing him. Then the helmet yoyoed back across the floorboards, wheeling past Dell's boots, colliding with a dressing table leg. But it might as well have wounded Dickens: he fell on his side, shielding his face, drawing himself into a ball. His chest heaved and a pitiful moan, punctuated with sobs, trembled out of him.

"Rotten!"

I covered my ears, gazing at Dell's mesh hood—which had dropped before me, had landed in a clump by the pallet—but I still heard everything.

"Doing that here!" she was yelling at him. "Bringing nasty nastiness into our home!" She turned, her housedress sweeping above her boots, and crouched in front of me: "This is my home! My home, betrayer! Like father like daughter, I'd say. That's right, of course!"

And I was a spy, she said so. I always went where I wasn't invited, bringing my little friends, my little spies.

"Watching in bushes, vile nasty child! You'll starve, right? No more food for you, not a thing, nothing!"

"I didn't do anything!" I said, and began crying. "I didn't do anything!"

"Liar!"

"I didn't—"

She grabbed my wrist and stared at Cut 'N Style, mocking me, saying, "I didn't do anything, I didn't do anything!"

"I didn't—"

Messing where I don't belong. Me and my friends.

"I've seen you do it, spying everywhere!"

On her land and in her home and being filthy with Dickens in Momma's room.

"You're not welcome here, wicked one!"

Now I'd starve. I'd wither and die. No more me. That's what she said.

"And no more of these—"

Then she shook my wrist, making Cut 'N Style wobble and fall from my finger.

"No more spies—"

She stood upright, crossing to the dressing table, where she opened a drawer and rifled about inside of it.

"Child, you're not the only one who lurks—"

Then she returned to me with something planted on a mittened index finger, something sprouting red hair; it was, I was horrified to discover, Classique.

"This is a troublesome creature," Dell told me, twitching Classique in front of my face so I could see her. "This is you—!"

"That's mine," I sobbed.

"No," Dell said, "I think not."

My guts twisted, my stomach roared with pain, as if Classique had been ripped from me.

"She's mine and I hate you!" I screamed. "I hate you, hate you—!"

I hate you!

And hearing my words, Dell's ferociousness crumbled into a stunned silence; she was taken aback, and—with Classique curling into a fist—she lowered her hand.

"What an awful thing to say," she said, sounding truly hurt. "What an awful, terrible thing to utter at someone."

With tears welling, snot dripping, I glared at her vexed, confused expression. Just then Dickens' heels banged the floorboards, his arms flailed. He wasn't moaning anymore, and, when I looked, he was on his back, convulsing wildly; spit bubbled between his clenched teeth, and his face strained as spasms jolted his body, as he hissed saliva and gagged.

"Look what you've done," Dell said, rushing to him. "Look what you've done!"

She pried his mouth open, forcing two fingers into his throat—Classique stuck on one of them, disappearing from sight again, lost in another hole. And I didn't understand why she was doing that, why she blamed me and was choking him with my doll head. All I knew was that I had to escape or next she'd be using those fingers on me, slipping them past my lips. So I sprang forward, grabbing the hood.

Without this you're dead, I thought. Without this bees will kill you good.

"Evil! Evil!"

And I was fast, much faster than Dell. I was a ghost, sailing around her outstretched arms, her clawing mittens.

"Monster child!"

I don't remember running from the witch's cave, or tearing along the footpath, passing the hole where Classique had fallen. I can't recall Dell's hood slipping from my hand, drifting to the ground behind me. Or scrambling across the tracks. Or locking the front door of What Rocks. Or crying as I told my father what happened.

But I did cry, weeping for what seemed hours, wetting my father's quilt with tears. And finally exhausted, I shivered beside him—the lipstick smeared across my chin, my stomach aching, my legs sore from running—hugging his rigid form, hoping he'd protect me from Dell.

"I didn't do anything," I said, again and again. "I didn't. Just kissed Dickens, that's all. I didn't do anything."

My poor husband, I thought. Poor Classique, poor blind Cut 'N Style. She got you all. I'm next. She hates me. When she knows the squirrel is gone, she'll destroy me for sure. She'll probably hang my head in her living room, or stick me on a shelf in the shed.

But there was nowhere to go. At night, bog men stirred in the attic and in the sorghum with Queen Gunhild. At night, Dell would wander outside, I knew. So how long did I have? How long until nightfall and the bees went to bed? That's when she'd come for me. Now she was in her cave, perhaps stuffing Dickens with wire, waiting for night. Then she'd arrive with her tools and buckets. She'd crash through the front door, yelling, "Filthy filthy!"

And lying with my father, I prayed for food and somewhere safe to hide. I imagined those cities at the bottom of the ocean, those castles and families–that's where I belonged. Classique would probably meet me there, so would Dickens and Cut 'N Style. My father was already dreaming himself there, I felt certain. And if I could only dream myself there too. If I could shut my eyes and try hard enough, I might find myself waking inside his dream.

If I tried hard enough, if I closed my eyes and held my breath–if I tried hard enough–

I never heard the breath leave my body. Before sleep, the last sound to fill my ears was the beating of my heart, and I knew I was slipping past the tideland, going beneath the ocean and sinking away from What Rocks. The afternoon light had faded above; maybe the waves had curled high enough to extinguish the sun. And in that far-flung region of my imagination, I tried understanding the exact circumstances that brought me to Texas instead of Denmark, but nothing presented itself. I knew only that I'd been on my own since that first night in the back country, and that I'd fled Los Angeles after my mother turned blue. Then I saw myself swimming through a vast underwater wilderness, going deeper and deeper, like a penny tossed into the Hundred Year Ocean–or Alice falling very slowly in the rabbit-hole, looking about, wondering what was going to happen next.

22

The end of the world was purple, appearing as an iris or a rose in my dream, blooming with an ear-piercing eruption, the petals suddenly bursting away from the bud like a firework. Or was I already half-awake–having just stirred beside my father–when the explosions shook What Rocks so abruptly, so violently, that the table lamp beside my bed fell to the floor; the window near the staircase collapsed in pieces, and all the windows downstairs–I soon discovered–shattered inward, throwing glass over the floorboards.

Then with astonishing speed, the ruinous aftermath of the blasts unfolded beyond the farmhouse, cacophonous and jarring–the whine of iron wheels sparking on the tracks, passenger cars tipping this way and that, metal striking metal, the ground quaking–then everything was quiet, enveloped in a brown and white dust which rose into the evening sky like smoke.

No, it isn't really the end of the world, I thought, only the end of the monster shark. But I wasn't certain, not there in my bedroom or downstairs or out on the porch. I wasn't certain until reaching the grazing pasture, where the derailment became apparent—the bus had been smashed beneath a top-pled passenger car, another car rested in Dell's meadow. Waning sunlight cut through the dust cloud, reflecting off the silver-tinted wreckage—and it seemed the entire train had turned edgeways, spilling cars on either side and across the rails, up and down the tracks, as far as the eye could see.

Then, in the stillness following the crash, I understood that Dickens killed the shark, that somehow he escaped Dell and her fingers. Now he was diving in Lisa, and if I sat and waited he would find me. He would emerge from the dust in his goggles and flip-flops, his lips puckered and ready for a kiss. And as the silence gave way to alarmed voices calling back and forth from within the passenger cars—as stunned men and women and children began climbing from the wreckage—I looked for him, searching the faces of those who staggered toward me.

At first just a few came, settling down in the pasture, speechless and seemingly uninjured, sitting upright with dazed expressions. But eventually the crowd grew in number, bringing both the wounded and the shocked—a young woman, pressing a bloody handkerchief over her mouth, held an infant to her breast; in front of her stood an elderly man, staring at the flattened, upturned bus, shaking his head in confusion as his left arm dangled limply. Others begged for water or help, some complained about the dust. Every so often I heard weeping, at times screaming. And the chaos swarming around and on the tracks—all those people running along the embankment, clamoring among the high weeds and foxtails—showed no signs of ending.

"Little girl—are you hurt anywhere?" said a woman. She was sitting nearby, cradling her purse in one arm. "Are you okay?"

Aside from a scratch on her cheek and disheveled hair, she appeared to have survived without serious injury. But her eyes were watery, her voice trembled when she spoke, and I noticed how she absently yanked bluebonnets, one after another, crushing the flowers firmly before dropping them.

"I'm just hungry is all," I told her. "I was sleeping."

And she flinched, as if my words had agitated her.

"Here, I have something." She opened her purse and pulled out an orange, asking, "Are you traveling alone or with someone?"

I shrugged.

"Don't know," I replied, my stomach grumbling while she peeled the fruit. "I guess Dickens will come get me, I'm pretty sure he will."

I watched as she rotated the orange, using her fingernails to scrape away the rind. Then she offered me the orange with a shaky hand, and instantaneously my teeth were on it.

"You're parents weren't on the train?"

I shook my head, chewing.

The woman's face twitched. I couldn't tell if she was smiling or frowning. She scooted closer, wrapping an arm across my shoulders, hugging me against her.

"It happened so fast," she said, nodding at the toppled passenger cars. "We're two of the lucky ones, thank God. We're very, very lucky."

But I didn't feel lucky; I was starving. And eating the orange, I continued looking for Dickens in the crowd, scanning the grim newcomers to the pasture. I kept imagining what it would be like to see him again, to find that he was all right.

Hello, Captain. You killed the shark. I love you.

All at once my eyes found a woman who, like the elderly man, seemed to be standing in a stupor. She was wearing a blue bathrobe, and her hair was covered with a clear-plastic shower cap. When she turned–glancing about frantically–I saw her face in the dusty evening light, and fear seized me.

"Dell," I mumbled, thoughtlessly biting into the orange.

She was shouting for Dickens, searching the crowd. And she was frightened, I could tell. Her fingers gripped the bathrobe, her fuzzy slippers trampled bluebonnets. She was so close that if I ran she'd surely spot me.

You'll stay far, I thought. You'll mess elsewhere.

And if my mouth wasn't full, I would've turned my head and spit.

But in the brief instant that I considered fleeing, Dell hurried off, moving toward the tracks, pushing through the throng of people. Then she vanished, disappearing somewhere among the wreckage.

"It's all right," the woman was saying. "We're safe now. We'll take care of each other, how's that? I'll make sure you get where you're going."

I wanted to say that there was nowhere else for me to go. I would've told her too, except the fireflies arrived. Dozens of tiny flashes materialized at once, swimming overhead—here, then gone, then there, gone—flashing in the thick dust, blink blink blinking in the pasture.

"They're so beautiful," I said. "They're my friends, you know. They have names."

And for a moment I forgot why I'd come to the pasture. I'd almost forgotten everything. I brought my head to the woman's breast, snuggling myself into her, and finished the orange—licking my lips after the last bite, aware of the lingering sweetness on my tongue and the stickiness on my chin—content as the fireflies welcomed the night.